The Long Chase

JACK GREENER

A Black Horse Western

ROBERT HALE · LONDON

ISBN 0 7090 7018 7

Robert Hale Limited
Clerkenwell House
Clerkenwell Green
London EC1R 0HT

Typeset by
Derek Doyle & Associates, Liverpool.
Printed and bound in Great Britain by
Antony Rowe Limited, Wiltshire.

Contents

1
The Big Fraud

''Who's next? Name?'

'Newton.'

Newt, now at the head of the queue, stepped up to the mark, calm and relaxed. There was just enough breeze to make him cautious as he raised his .22 hunting rifle to take a careful sighting. Target shooting was no more difficult than shooting for the pot – with the advantage that a target did not move at the critical moment. Even as a boy he'd had the knack of straight shooting.

The watching crowd fell silent. Holding his breath until he was sure of his aim, and rock-steady, Newt focused his attention on the distant target. Unhurriedly he squeezed off a shot, another, and then a third.

His finger released its pressure on the trigger and he took air into his lungs in a long, steady breath while he waited for the judge's decision.

One of the onlookers whistled. 'Now that's what I call grouping!'

The judge, a greying man in buckskins, with untrimmed whiskers, walked up to the target and studied it closely.

Overhead a wide canvas banner flapped loosely; it bore the painted words: Golden Pacific Railroad.

The judge said, 'Well shot, Mr Newton. An expert might equal that – I don't see how anyone else could beat it.'

The shooting match continued and bets were laid. A trestle-table had been set up on wasteland just beyond the end of Damwell's main thoroughfare to sell beer and spirits, chops and pies. Newt bought a pork pie and moved into the shade as the queue shortened. Some contestants fancied themselves as gunslingers, others were so wildly off-target as to suggest they'd had a drink too many.

Newt watched the short man with a shock of white hair who'd sponsored the prize: a shiny new Colt .44 revolver. He wore a beaming smile and carried excess weight; a fashionable coat fitted tightly over his swelling paunch. Apparently he was a railroad promoter known as 'Doc' Solomon. After charging fifty cents' entry fee, this promotion wasn't going to break Golden Pacific – especially if Colt was providing the weapon as an advertisement.

Newt was no taller, but thin as a beanpole, and nowhere near as young as he seemed. His farm-clothes were clean, but patched, and he was aware he looked a bit ridiculous in his old felt hat.

The line of would-be sharpshooters finally ended.

The judge called for silence. 'I declare the winner to be Mr Newton.'

There were cheers, moans, and a few glasses raised. Solomon bustled forward, ruddy face jovial, puffing on an expensive cigar.

'Well done, young man. I have much pleasure in presenting you with this magnificent new revolver, courtesy of Golden Pacific Railroad.' He handed Newt the Colt with a flourish. 'And now, if you please, a photograph for our publicity department …'

A man pushed through the crowd and set up a tripod with a plate camera on top. He placed Newt carefully at a measured distance and a couple of helpers held up a white sheet behind him.

'Now sir, if you'll just hold your prize in front of you, and keep absolutely still for three minutes …'

Newt remained patient until his picture had been taken.

Solomon rubbed his hands together, smiling. 'Excellent, excellent. As well as your prize, Mr Newton, I can offer you a job, starting at a dollar a day and all the grub you can eat – you're a quiet one and I like that – as a guard to protect my graders and track-layers when we penetrate Indian country. Everyone calls me "Doc" and I hope you will too.'

'A dollar a day?'

Newt kept his face carefully blank; he'd imagined that a railroad would pay more than the rate any man could get selling his labour.

'To start, to start,' Solomon said quickly. 'There's no

9

telling where this job might take you.' He winked. 'My train's just leaving. Hop aboard and enjoy a free ride to the end of the track. Introduce yourself to Cass, my chief guard – he'll fix you up.' He clapped a shiny top hat on his head.

Newt nodded. 'I'll do that, Mr Solomon.'

The railroad boss paused as he turned to move away. 'Doc, call me Doc.'

Newt walked to the depot where a locomotive hitched to a single carriage had steam up. He was beginning to reconsider the wisdom of leaving home. At least he ate regularly on the farm; but he'd got the itch to be a cowboy and, one day, own his own ranch. He aimed to rope steers and take a herd to a cow town, to have his own brand and spurs that jingled.

He stepped up alongside the locomotive, the Colt stuck in his belt, and carrying his .22 rifle. The engineer appeared amused.

'You can ride in the cab with me,' he called, and Newt climbed up.

The engineer blew the whistle and eased off the brake.

The train moved away, rattling and shaking. Newt expected it to speed up, but it maintained its steady progress, not much faster than a horse.

After a while they reached a wooden trestle-bridge spanning a gorge; the gap wasn't wide but it was deep. The engineer took the crossing even more slowly, and Newt looked at him.

'When you see the outfit working for us, you'll

figure it out,' the engineer said.

'That so?'

The train rumbled along and Newt thought, at least it's travelling west. Eventually they arrived at the rail-head and he jumped down.

'Thanks for the ride.'

Newt looked about him. Work was proceeding in a casual manner; graders levelled the ground and men laid rails and spiked them. Watching, he thought it would take a long time for this track to reach wherever it was going. Solomon's outfit appeared ridiculously small and easygoing; the 'Pacific' in the title seemed wildly optimistic.

He saw a man cooking over a fire and beyond him a few tents, iron rails, hammers and spikes.

'I'm looking for Cass,' he called to a man leaning on a shovel.

The workman glanced at the shiny new revolver stuck in Newt's belt.

'New guard, huh?' he said, and spat on the ground. Then he glanced around. 'He's coming now.'

Newt saw a big man carrying a rifle. He wore two holstered revolvers and a heavy moustache.

'Reckon you're the new guard, right? Every time we hit a small town, Doc pulls this stunt.'

Curious, Newt asked, 'Is he really a doctor?'

The chief guard snorted. 'You wouldn't want him operating on you. Forget the "Doc" – that's short for Caradoc – he's Mr Solomon to you, same as I'm Mr Cassidy.'

He glared at the man holding a shovel. 'If you're tired, I'll dig a grave for yuh to lie in.'

The workman moved away, and Cassidy said, 'The boss talks big to get financing – but this is only a spur line. Forget his spiel about Indian territory; your job is to guard railroad property. Some of the shirkers we've got can't wait for pay day – they sneak off, helping themselves to tools and any loose equipment they can carry. A thieving lot. When someone quits, you make sure they leave empty-handed.'

'When do guards get paid?'

'Once a month. Did the boss say anything about investors coming out to see how we're doing?'

Newt raised an eyebrow. 'Not to me.'

'Any time they do, get busy. Understand? We've got to look like we're aiming to build clear to the west coast. Our chief engineer's a drunk so take no notice of what he says. Go see the cookie and take a nap. I'm putting you on night duty – stay awake and see no one walks off with railroad property.'

'Sure thing, Mr Cassidy.'

'Leave that .22 behind. Use your revolver – a .44 slug will stop 'em dead.'

Cookie was neither friendly nor unfriendly; he just regarded the newcomer as one more mouth to feed. Newt had no problem sleeping; he found a patch of shade and curled up. His last thought was about how long he'd stay; this job obviously didn't hold much future for a would-be cattle baron....

When he woke the night air was still warm, the

shadows dark. The camp was silent, and stars showed briefly between drifting banks of cloud.

Newt stretched and began his night patrol, moving carefully between stacks of iron rails and spikes. There were shovels and hammers piled up near the tents; snores but no lights came from the tents.

He was still puzzled by the lack of activity; it seemed the men had packed up work early and bedded down.

He appeared to be the only night guard, and assumed the new man always drew that duty. Well, it would be no hardship to wing a bullet past the ear of any casual thief.

Voices drifted on the night air, and he paused. The smell of cigar smoke reached him, and he guessed the railroad boss had arrived before he recognized his voice. Doc Solomon had a distinctive boom to his voice that carried.

'Stop worrying, Cass. There's nobody in these hick towns sharp enough to see we take on a guard only to throw dust in their faces. As long as we keep the track moving along, laying a few rails, and a loco runs now and then, we're safe enough. When I chair a meeting, I always emphasize our difficulties – that it'll take a bit more money to push the track further. Always that bit more money!' He chuckled.

Newt was poised, one foot in the air. He knew he shouldn't be listening to a private conversation, and was preparing to back away – but he froze as Cassidy answered.

'It's called fraud, Doc, and that means a term in jail

13

if someone catches on. I don't think you'd like it in a prison cell, with none of those little luxuries you enjoy. Why don't we quit while we're ahead? You must have a quarter-million salted away by now.'

'You'll get your share, Cass, so stop worrying.'

'I'm not worried exactly, it's just—'

Newt's boot came down on a tin can.

Solomon whirled about as the moon came from behind a cloud. 'It's that damned kid I picked for guard. Nail him, Cass!'

Solomon's voice no longer held a chuckle, but had an undertone of menace.

Cass turned, drawing a revolver.

It was automatic. Faced with a man drawing on him, Newt whipped the new Colt from his belt, aimed instinctively and squeezed the trigger. Flame stabbed the night; the shot sounded loud in the silence.

A red stain blossomed on Cassidy's shirt front, plumb centre; his mouth opened in a wheeze as he staggered from the shock. He went down on his back and didn't move again.

Solomon looked as if he couldn't believe his eyes. He yelled, 'Help! Murder! I'll put the law on you for this!'

As the camp came to life, Newt turned and ran, fading into the night.

2
Bridge Burning

Newt was not happy. He stumbled among shadowy trees, pausing to listen from time to time. He made some effort to move quietly, but pursuit seemed to have ended and he was alone. Once he got beyond the canopy of leaves he took his direction from the stars and headed back towards Damwell. The night grew colder.

His dream of becoming a cowboy and, eventually, running his own ranch had turned sour. He'd killed a man and been called 'murderer'. He wondered how far Solomon would go. Obviously there was something fraudulent going on that the railroad promoter wouldn't want exposed – and who would bother to investigate Golden Pacific if the only witness was a hunted criminal?

In his dream world, he would just ride off on his horse. But Newt was on foot and had only a few dollars in his pocket. Already he felt hungry. He needed a meal and a horse – and he knew what it meant to be branded a horse-thief. He'd left his .22 rifle back at the rail-camp too.

He reached the trestle-bridge as first light came and had just crossed it when he heard the rumble of iron wheels behind him. He left the track and got under cover till the train passed.

Some time later he approached a small town warily. He hadn't noticed a town marshal or deputy sheriff in his brief visit, but kept to back alleys. He found a small café and ordered bacon with beans and coffee.

Nobody challenged him, so obviously word hadn't got around yet. The talk was of Doc Solomon's horse – apparently a mare – being matched against a local champion in a race.

'Those Indian horses aren't really fast,' one man insisted. 'I know where my money's going.'

'Fast enough,' another replied, 'and a horse that will last. I'd bet on Doc's mount if it's going to be a distance race. Looks good too.'

'Looks ain't anything.'

Newt paid for his meal and walked casually along to the corner with Main Street; stores were opening and, outside one, a man was using a hammer to tack up a sheet of paper. After he'd gone, Newt strolled up to read the notice.

With a shock, he saw a picture of his own face looking back at him; it must have been printed from the photograph taken after the shooting match.

The picture was printed beneath a heading in bold capitals: WANTED! Under his likeness he read:

This young man, calling himself Newton, is wanted for the murder of a railroad guard. He is armed and dangerous. A reward of $100 is offered for his capture dead or alive.

> C. Solomon, Managing Director
> Golden Pacific Railroad.

Newt was stunned. Solomon wasn't going to let it go; the railroad promoter intended to shut his mouth permanently.

Newt turned away, troubled. A murderer, with a price on his head. That was bad enough but, if word of this got back to his family … he winced at the idea. They would be ashamed.

Mother might not believe the charge, but Father would sigh and shake his head and mutter, 'This is what comes of leaving home.' Newt had waited till his brother was old enough to take over his chores about the farm; Russ would be angry and hotheaded enough to go gunning for someone. Sis would turn red and avoid her friends.

Newt had been brought up to value honesty and now this, through no fault of his own. Solomon had something to answer for.

He turned into an alley, walking on the shadowed side, his mind numb. He had a little time before word got around, and he tried to think what was the best thing to do, but his ideas seemed stuck in a groove and the answer always came out the same; he needed a horse to get away fast.

Then he remembered Doc Solomon's mare and his lips thinned in a tight smile. The phrase 'poetic justice' popped into his head.

First he needed information and, having taken his decision, he walked boldly into the nearest store. It was not yet busy, but word had already beaten him there.

The storekeeper, stooped with age and sparse of hair, placed his empty hands on the counter. 'No need for shooting,' he said. 'I ain't no hero – just take what's in the till.'

'I just want a little information,' Newt said politely. 'Heard talk about a horse-race, matching this mare of Doc Solomon.'

'Guess that's off now,' the storekeeper said. 'The last I heard, Doc had invited some bigwigs out to the end of track, and his horse was going along with them.'

'That sounds interesting,' Newt drawled, remembering the wooden bridge. 'I suppose you sell kerosene?'

''Course I do. Look, I'm not going to start any trouble. Take all the fuel you need.'

'Reckon a gallon will do, with an old rag and some matches.'

The storekeeper filled his order promptly, keeping his hands in full view. 'There's no charge to you, Mr Newton.'

'Well, thanks.'

As Newt left by the door, he heard the storekeeper

18

give a sigh of relief and sit down. He started walking towards the railroad track, carrying his can of oil; and it occurred to him that there were advantages to having a price on his head.

It was too hot to hurry, even though he didn't know how long he'd got, but he heard nothing coming up behind him. He kept walking along the track.

When finally he reached the bridge across the gorge, he took time to study it carefully. He laid a hand on the woodwork and found it warm to the touch, and dry. It hadn't rained for several weeks.

The bridge should go fast, he thought, once it caught alight. He uncapped the can of kerosene, soaked the rag to use as a fuse and tied the rag to the nearest support. He poured he rest of the can over wooden struts and chucked the empty can into the gulch.

He struck a match. The fuel-soaked rag caught alight immediately and flared up. Newt fanned the flame with his old felt hat to get a draught going, then had to back away as a wave of heat came from the burning wood. The fire spread quickly and it was obvious the bridge would no longer bear the weight of a locomotive.

He walked back along the track, listening.

He heard a distant whistle and, presently, the rails began to hum. Newt stood beside the track and, when he saw the train approaching, waved his arms vigorously as a warning.

The locomotive, now pulling two carriages, came nearer, belching smoke. The wheels began to turn more slowly and the engineer leaned from the cab. 'What is it, feller?'

'The bridge is alight,' Newt yelled. 'It's not safe to cross.'

The engineer applied the brake and the train gradually rolled to a standstill. He got down and walked forward to see for himself.

The first carriage held Solomon's potential backers. The second was a baggage van and Newt walked up to this and opened the door.

A horse stood there, regarding him with bright-eyed interest. She was taller than the usual cow-pony, and distinguished by dappled white markings on a grey body. The legs looked strong.

'You're a beaut,' Newt murmured, running a hand over her as he untied a rope and led the mare down a ramp. She came willingly enough.

A few passengers followed the engineer towards the bridge over the gorge, which was now burning furiously. Others drifted back to the baggage van to watch Newt with the mare.

'That's Solomon's horse,' one said.

'Was,' Newt replied casually, carrying a saddle from the van and slapping it over the mare's back. She gave the impression she was eager to be away after being cooped up in the van.

Another man said, 'You're stealing that horse – and I know who you are. I saw the poster in Damwell. You're a convicted killer!'

'Not convicted,' Newt corrected.

A third passenger said, 'He saved our lives, you know, by stopping the train.'

An argument commenced, but no one appeared anxious to take a more active role. Perhaps they had observed Newt's marksmanship.

Newt got the saddle girth tightened to his satisfaction, swung up and rode off.

Behind him, a passenger shook his head. 'Doc ain't going to like this.'

Caradoc Solomon strode up and down the end of the rail-camp in a black mood. The men kept their backs to him and tried to look as if they were working. He was scared because a witness who knew too much about him was running loose; furious because that same someone had stolen his favourite mare.

He glowered at the soggy end of a cigar he'd chewed to a ruin and flung it away. Potential backers who could have been persuaded to invest money in his railroad had not arrived. He had the extra cost of rebuilding a bridge, and he had to replace Cassidy – with no help from the mare who had won big money for him at the races.

He promised that Newton would curse the day he'd won that Colt revolver.

Solomon continued to pace up and down, unsmiling, without a chuckle in him, his voice no longer soft. He scowled at his workmen and swore at them. They worked reluctantly and he knew, as soon as he turned his back, they'd down tools.

He needed a hard man to run this end of things. His magic touch belonged in towns and cities, milking money from those who hoped to get rich quick, a touch that never failed.

But first he had to deal with Newton. That one had made a mistake in stealing the mare; the name of 'horse-thief' meant a quick hanging job – Westerners didn't waste time on judge and jury when it was a matter of horseflesh.

After a time, he calmed sufficiently to sit down with pencil and paper to rewrite his reward poster. And he put the reward money up to 200 dollars.

He hesitated over mentioning the mare – but realized he'd have to take the risk. It was his best chance to rid himself permanently of Newton.

He wrote HORSETHIEF in bold capitals as the heading for his new posters, and smiled. Doc Solomon didn't think Newton would be running around loose for much longer, not after this notice circulated.

3
A Wall of Sheep

The mare moved along as if she had wings, head up and nostrils flared, her hoofs barely seeming to touch the ground. She carried Newt as though he were no more than a feather on her back. Her legs pistoned effortlessly as she headed for the horizon. Damwell was left miles behind and still she moved like a champion.

'Maybe you know something, gal,' Newt murmured. 'Maybe you, too, have a reason to get away from Solomon ... in the Old Testament, Solomon was a wise man. Waal, I reckon you're a wise horse so I'll name you Sheba, you being a queen among horses and, as I recall, the Queen of Sheba left Solomon flat after a brief visit.'

He let the mare set her own pace and she covered the ground steadily. When darkness came she halted amongst long grass beside a stream and Newt removed the saddle to use as a pillow. They both drank from the stream and she grazed beneath the stars while he slept under a leafy tree.

Newt woke early and splashed water over his face.

Sheba had wandered during the night so he put his fingers in his mouth and gave a long shrill whistle. It was answered by a thudding of hoofs as the mare galloped up. Her muzzle nudged him.

'Guess you want your breakfast, gal.'

As he saddled up he felt reassured because the mare had answered his call. He set off, following the stream to a small town. At the livery barn he ordered a mixture of hay and oats for her.

The stablehand regarded the mare with admiration. 'Sure plenty horse there, mister. D'you ever race her?'

'Not interested,' Newt said briefly.

He walked out and found a small diner for his own breakfast. Solomon's poster hadn't reached here yet, but he could see another problem: Sheba was too easily recognized.

As they jogged out of town, Newt reflected that his remaining money wasn't going to stretch far now it had to feed two. But he had to keep moving, so he needed the mare. He couldn't take a job that involved staying in one place, so . . .

'Looks like I'll have to earn our keep as a gun for hire,' he murmured, 'but who needs to hire a gun?'

The sun rose higher and the grassed prairie passed at a steady pace. Once he saw cattle in the distance, and turned away to avoid the riders; before he would have been thrilled to meet real cowboys.

As they travelled through a valley with a steep cliff on one side, Sheba shied. For the first time, Newt found her reluctant to advance.

He heard a shot, and then another. A cloud of buzzards rose and circled overhead.

Further ahead lay what appeared to be a grey wall. He sat watching, puzzled, for a few minutes but there seemed to be no immediate danger so he stroked Sheba's neck and talked quietly to her and she went forward slowly.

Then he saw the wall was a mass of sheep piled high; apparently dead except for one or two. A lone figure on foot moved among them, shooting those still alive.

Newt advanced cautiously. The figure with the rifle turned to face him, gun coming up to cover him.

He realized, late, that he was looking at a woman, solidly built and wearing a man's working-clothes. Her nut-brown face showed strain; her lips pressed into a tight line as she watched him.,

After a few seconds, she called out: 'If you're a cowboy, turn around and get outa here.'

'Sure got a hankering to be a cowboy, ma'am, but I can't claim to be one as yet.'

The rifle-barrel lowered a fraction. 'Luckily for you, mister.'

Newt edged Sheba gently forward.

'I'm about done here,' she said bitterly. 'I've finished off the injured – there's not one I could save.'

'An accident? Disease?'

'No accident – a disease called cattlemen. God, how I hate those bastards!'

Newt was shocked. Ever since he was a boy and had

heard tales of the adventures of wild and reckless cowboys, he'd longed to be one. He'd envied them their carefree life – now he faced a woman who hated the breed.

'I don't …'

She pointed up to the cliff top. 'That's my land up there. Johnson wants it for his cattle – so he and his cowboys drove our flock off the cliff … I've been putting down the injured survivors.'

Newt felt embarrassed. Nothing was turning out the way he'd imagined. His dream was turning into a nightmare. He looked at her tear-stained face. 'You alone, ma'am?'

'I am now. Johnson's hired gunman murdered my husband, Tom.'

'Sure sorry, ma'am,' he muttered – and wondered if he'd really intended to hire out his gun. Widow-making was not a career he fancied.

She gave him a long look. 'That's enough of my troubles. I can give yuh a meal if you ride up to my shack at the top. Name's Lane – Mrs Lane, as was.'

She couldn't keep the sadness out of her voice, and he replied,

'Newt, ma'am.'

She collected her horse and started up. Newt turned Sheba's head towards a steep path and slowly followed her to the top of the cliff.

There was only one hotel in Damwell and Solomon had commandeered the largest room. He sat in a padded chair, a glass of brandy in one hand and a cigar in the other, nervously watching the man opposite him.

He had an uneasy feeling this meeting was not a good idea but it was too late to back out. He'd made his bid, and waited to hear Ballew's reply.

'Cigar?' he offered again. 'A drink of some kind?'

'I don't smoke, and rarely drink when I'm working.' The voice held a Southern drawl overlaid with a veneer of ice.

Ballew had a reputation as a gun for hire. He commanded respect and top money. He sat on a hard chair with his back to a wall, a position from which he could see Solomon, the door and the window.

He wore a business-suit, the coat open, the first finger of his right hand tapping absently on the butt of the revolver holstered at his hip. Long hair straggled from under the back of a derby hat. When he spoke, he kept his gaze fixed on Solomon's face.

'Five hundred cash, now.'

'I don't carry that kind of money on me.'

'You can get it from the bank.'

Solomon knew it would be useless to deny it. 'Five hundred,' he agreed. 'I want Newton dead and the horse – discreetly – returned to me.'

'Something about the horse?'

Solomon cursed silently; this man was sharp as well as deadly. He nodded. 'When you're successful, there's a job waiting for yuh, running my railroad camp – with a share in the profits.'

Ballew stared at him. 'Maybe,' he drawled. 'A man in my trade likes the idea of retiring in style, with that extra bit of comfort.'

Solomon mopped the sweat from his forehead, and relaxed. He'd got what he wanted, even if it had cost more than he wanted to pay. Sometimes you had to pay extra to stay in the game.

His cherubic smile returned; Newton was no more than a walking dead man.

The shepherd's hut was built of logs, rough-hewn outside but comfortable within. The land was well grassed and Newt could see how a cattleman would want it. He unsaddled Sheba and turned her loose to graze.

He sat in a plain wood chair and sipped hot coffee, black, sweet and strong, watching the widow Lane busy at the stove; she appeared restless and unable to settle. She kept on the move, never far from her rifle as she cooked meat and vegetables. Keeping on the move seemed to be her way of coping with catastrophe so he didn't offer to help.

When the meal was ready they sat at table together; a stranger could have assumed they were man and wife. The meat was lamb, the vegetables, potatoes and onions, were grown on a cultivated patch just outside; the bread was home baked and cut into large chunks. There was water in a jug.

Lane studied him thoughtfully. 'You look like you might be a farmer.'

'Was. I left home with the idea of becoming a cowboy but it went wrong.'

'That's life, I guess. Things going wrong.' Tears rolled down her cheeks as she ate. 'It could have been a good life.' Bitterness crept into her voice. 'Always some bastard to spoil it. Always.'

She ate furiously, as if eating could wipe out the past. 'What went wrong for you?'

'I'm on the run, after I killed a man.'

'I feel like killing one myself.'

Abruptly she got up, washed her face and ran a comb through her hair. She studied her face in a piece of mirror. 'No sense letting myself go.'

He saw she was younger than he'd first thought; in a store dress she'd make a picture.

'Is there no law around here?' Newt asked.

'There's a sheriff at Yuba, our local town, but Johnson owns him. Like he owns everything else, and what he doesn't own, he takes.'

'Doesn't seem right somehow.'

She gave him a pitying look, as if to say: how old are you?

Hoofbeats sounded faintly, a tattoo of drumbeats racing closer. Voices shouted, 'Yippee-ii!' Laughter echoed. The riders circled the house and then fell silent.

A quiet voice said, 'Strange horse, boss.'

'I see it.'

Lane picked up her rifle. 'That'll be Johnson and his crew.'

Newt pushed back his chair and went to the door. He opened it, Colt stuck in his belt, and saw a half-circle of mounted cowboys.

The big man on a stallion glared down at him. 'Where the hell did you spring from? Who are yuh? What are you doing here?'

Newt ignored him. Most of the men looked like ordinary cowhands. 'Never heard tell of cowboys making war on a woman before,' he said quietly.

Some eyes were lowered. A few riders backed off. One muttered, 'Just following the boss's orders.'

The big man blustered. 'Move away, feller, or we'll bury yuh here.'

'Is that why you've brought your army? Big feller like you could sure handle one woman on his own.'

For a moment, Newt thought the rancher might explode and that would have made a mess of his embroidered shirt. His face crimsoned, then he lifted a big Stetson and wiped the sweat band.

'Don't get me riled, son. I'm Johnson and my word is law around here. The woman is moving out. She won't be harmed, but the shack is going to burn. I won't stand for sheep or sheep-lovers on my land.'

From behind Newt, Mrs Lane said defiantly, 'It's my land, and I'm staying.'

Johnson turned his head to look at the rider next to him. 'Heff, take care of the man.'

The cowboy was black as a coal-heaver. White teeth shone as he smiled his satisfaction. 'My pleasure, Mr Johnson.'

He swung down from his saddle, wearing two revolvers.

Newt felt a distinct chill. He wondered if Heff was out to make his name as a mankiller; or maybe he had something against white folk and was just looking for an excuse, with Johnson offering a safe harbour. He might be fast, but Newt was accurate.

He said mildly, 'Not unless you're ready to join that heavenly choir.'

The negro hesitated. Newt began to count the riders backing Johnson. Behind him, Mrs Lane hissed, 'Remove the king-pin and the rest will collapse like a pricked balloon.'

It made sense. As Heff grabbed two-handed for his revolvers, Newt had his Colt lined up. He squeezed the trigger.

Johnson made a grunting noise and a red stain spoilt his fancy shirt; he slumped sideways and would have hit the ground, but his boots stayed in the stirrups.

Heff froze and his eyes bulged in disbelief. 'You've killed the boss!'

Newt said, 'So there's no point now, is there? He won't be paying yuh.' His gaze moved over Johnson's cowhands. 'Same applies, guess. Suggest you take care of the man's cattle and leave the lady be.'

Mrs Lane stepped up beside him, her rifle trained on the black cowboy.

'I know you're only a gun for your boss, Mr Heffner – but if I see yuh around here again I'll be remembering it was your finger on the trigger. Now git!'

31

One by one, the cowhands drifted away, leading Johnson's horse. Only the black man looked back, his expression poisonous.

4

The Horse that Changed

The Johnson riders split up. A few, towing the big man's stallion with his body tied in place, headed for the ranch house. Others were in favour of quitting and moving on. Heffner rode apart from both groups.

The crew had never liked him, even as a working cowhand; when he was promoted to Johnson's top gunhand, they left him strictly alone. It hit him in his wallet that the big boss wouldn't be paying him any more, and he lagged behind, trying to decide what would be the best thing for him to do.

His horse seemed to have an idea of its own and veered towards the trail leading to Yuba. Heffner shrugged; town was as good as any place right now. Maybe the sheriff would have something to say; after all, he had been Johnson's man too. When it occurred to him it might be to his advantage to get his version in first, he used his spurs. As he rode, he thought about how he'd tell it.

The straggly line of shacks marking Yuba's main street showed and he pushed his mount to a brisk trot, swung from the saddle outside the law-office and hitched. He strode inside like a man with urgent business.

Sheriff Walsh sat at ease behind his desk, using a toothpick; an elderly man, grey-haired from experience.

He glanced at the black man without expression or greeting. 'Have yuh got a message for me from the boss?'

Heffner showed gleaming teeth in a smile. 'Mr Johnson is sure enough dead.' He remained standing in front of Walsh, hat in hand.

'Dead? How come? Are you telling it straight, Heff?'

'Stranger shot him when he didn't even have a gun in his hand. Murder, clear enough.'

Walsh's eyes got a keen light in them. 'Where was this? And where were you?'

'At the sheepwoman's place. She had a stranger with her. Soon as the boss spoke to her, this feller drew his gun and shot Mr Johnson through the heart. I saw it all, but I wasn't expecting anything like that, Mr Walsh.'

The sheriff sat motionless, staring at him.

Heff volunteered: 'Reckon that sheepwoman sure enough hired him to kill the boss, 'cause she was squatting on his land.'

Walsh grunted. 'Maybe. You seen this stranger before? Hear a name mentioned?'

'No sir.'

'Maybe I ought to ride out to the ranch, hear what some of the others have to say.'

Heffner could read Walsh's mind more easily than he could a newspaper; in his young days, guessing the mind of a white master was a survival skill. Now it was obvious that Walsh was wondering how long he'd stay sheriff without Johnson's backing.

'Maybe you ought to bring in that she-bitch and jail her. It's likely enough the feller she hired has moved on by this time.'

'And maybe not,' Walsh said. He was feeling his age and reluctant to face a man-killer.

Heffner waited patiently, his face carefully blank. Walsh represented the law so he'd have to do something. It remained to see what.

His wait was interrupted by a stranger walking through the doorway. Heffner stiffened. He knew a dangerous man when he saw one, and this man wore a single revolver under the open coat of a business-suit. Long hair stuck out from under the back of his derby.

The stranger ignored him and spoke directly to Walsh. That was all right; Heffner was used to being ignored; in the old days a black was always ignored as long as he obeyed orders.

'Have you seen this man, Sheriff?' The stranger pulled a poster from an inside pocket of his coat and unfolded it.

'Can't say I have,' Walsh admitted.

'I'm told he rides a mare, grey with white markings.'

Heffner remembered the strange horse at the sheepwoman's hut and moved around to look at the wanted man's picture.

'That's him!' he exclaimed. 'That's the one who killed Mr Johnson.'

The stranger looked at him. 'Killed? That makes his second murder, Sheriff. I figure he's on his way to carve a name for himself unless we stop him pronto.'

Walsh nodded. 'Guess I'll get a posse together – then we'll ride out to the Lane place.'

Heffner struggled with the words beneath the picture; it was at times like this he regretted his lack of an education. 'Reward' was plain enough, and excited him.

'Do we need a posse, Mr Walsh? Maybe the three of us can turn the trick – there's only a woman besides this Newton.'

The sheriff appealed to the stranger. 'What d'you think, Mr...?'

'Ballew's the name.'

'Mr Ballew. Guess you know more about Newton, than we do.'

Ballew nodded slightly. 'It's possible I do, Sheriff.' He gave the matter some thought. 'My advice is, form your posse and we'll all ride together.'

Heffner was disappointed. Sheriff Walsh got to his feet.

'I'll organize some men. I suggest that you, Mr

Ballew, rest up and take a meal on board. I can recommend the Surprise dining-rooms.'

He ignored the black man.

The widow Lane pointed across the valley. 'That way's the ranch house and river.' She shifted her position slightly and pointed again. 'And over there's our local town – Yuba.' She paused, looking intently at him. 'But you don't have to leave yet, do yuh?'

Newt hesitated. 'What will you do, ma'am?'

'I'm staying. I've still some money in the bank. As soon as I can get the beginnings of a flock together, I'll be back in business.'

He sighed. 'I guess being a shepherd, and stubborn, go together.'

'No cowboy's going to run me off my land.'

They were high up, looking out over the range, and Newt had to admit it was good land. Their horses grazed among trees and the air was clear and warm; there was even a slight breeze.

Newt got the impression she was making an offer, and had to admit he was stirred. In other circumstances he would have been tempted to stay, but he couldn't forget there was a price on his head. Sooner or later the law would catch up.

'Maybe I'll ride …'

He broke off as he saw dust rising on the trail from Yuba; riders heading towards them. He guessed that one of Johnson's men had been into town, and that this was a posse coming.

'Got to ride, ma'am,' he said, pointing down. 'Looks like trouble on its way.'

Lane studied the trail. 'Someone's been telling tales to the sheriff. Waal, I guess I'll have a different story to tell.'

'I'll still be on a Wanted poster.'

She nodded. 'You're right, of course.' She regarded him carefully. 'Our clothes are sufficiently different – especially that hat.'

'So?'

'We'll change clothes. Strip off … I'll lead them away while you hide among the trees. They'll only catch a glimpse of me – and that'll give you time to get clear away.'

Newt hesitated as she started to pull off her shirt.

'You shy or something? Remember I've been married and there's nothing you've got I ain't seen already. Now get out of those clothes in a hurry and into mine before they get close.'

Embarrassed, Newt turned his back to avoid staring at white flesh as she undressed. He handed her his shirt and pants and grabbed hers, dressing hastily. Her clothes had a woman smell that tickled his nose and made him sneeze.

'I won't forget this, ma'am,' he mumbled as she stuck his old felt hat on her head and tucked long hair underneath.

She swung into her saddle. 'Get under cover till they're past you.' She waved once and urged her horse into motion.

Newt led Sheba deeper among the trees and held her muzzle. 'Quiet, gal,' he murmured.

Lane's horse was going like a Fourth of July rocket and the posse swept by, riding hard. In the lead was an elderly man wearing a law badge; and beside him the black cowboy, Heffner. A man in a suit and wearing a derby tailed them and Newt wondered who he was.

He waited until the sound of pursuit died, then mounted, rode down into the valley and urged Sheba into the river. The mare wasn't afraid of water and went in without hesitation, swimming strongly.

Newt, in the saddle, breathed deep of air that had the taste of freedom. Water came up to his thighs as they were swept downstream.

Sheba climbed the far bank and shook herself before going on. Her long legs stretched and she gave the impression she was determined to see what lay beyond the horizon.

'Guess you just like running,' Newt murmured. 'It comes natural to yuh.'

She kept going at an easy loping pace until, when they reached a stand of trees, Newt reined her back. Screened from view he dismounted, removed the saddle and used bunches of dry grass to wipe her down.

It was then he noticed the smears. Alarmed he looked more closely at her hair, afraid she had suffered some injury.

But the mare was unharmed. Puzzled, he wiped the palm of his hand over a white patch of hair that had changed – and something came off on his hand. He continued rubbing down until all her markings vanished.

'Waal, I figure you ain't got no fancy dappling after all, Sheba – must have been some kind of dye and it's washed off.'

Sheba, now a grey mare, grazed contentedly, and Newt thought about it.

It seemed obvious that Doc Solomon had more than one swindle going. Running a horse under false markings and, he supposed, a false name, indicated the grey mare was known. Likely Doc had betted heavily on her to win.

And a crook like that had got him running for his life. Newt promised himself that one day there would be a reckoning.

He slapped Sheba on the rump and saddled her. 'Guess you really are a champ, gal.'

As he rode away he wondered if Mrs Lane was still fooling the posse.

Ballew rode at the back of the posse. He was a methodical man and his method, always, was to let others take the risk, then move in for the kill and collect the reward.

He was a careful man; after all, in his trade there was considerable risk, and he intended to live into a comfortable old age. He was acutely aware that many man-killers died young.

So he was coming up last of the bunch when their

quarry stopped in the open and turned to face them. The first thing he noticed was that they had been chasing the wrong horse. The posse churned around the lone rider as she removed an old hat and shook out her hair.

Sheriff Walsh swore. Heffner looked vicious. Ballew gave a small slow smile of appreciation.

'You're a damn fool, ma'am,' Walsh said. 'You could have got yourself shot.'

Suddenly the woman had a rifle in her hands, swinging the barrel to point at the black man. 'I warned you, Mr Heffner, if I ever saw yuh again I'd kill yuh.'

Heffner quickly manoeuvred his horse behind that of the sheriff.

She said calmly, 'He murdered my husband, Sheriff. Shot him down without giving him a chance. Are you going to take him in?'

'I've only your word for that, ma'am,' Walsh said uneasily, looking down the barrel of her rifle, 'So put that gun down. If you kill Heff in front of me, I'll have to arrest yuh.'

This sheriff, Ballew thought, was unhappy. 'Your posse still chasing Newton?' he asked, sitting quietly on his horse. His quarry had, for the moment vanished.

'There's no point,' Walsh said. 'He's outside my jurisdiction by now … think I'll take a ride over to Johnson's ranch to see what's happening there.'

The posse divided, a few going with Walsh, the

majority heading back to Yuba to slake their thirst. The widow Lane glared at Heffner.

'Keep riding, black boy. If I see yuh again, the sheriff may not be around for you to hide behind.'

She finally decided to go into town too, and Ballew and Heffner were left on their own.

Heffner was angry. 'The sheriff should have jailed her. She fooled us and let Newton get away. What I'd like to do …'

Ballew turned cold grey eyes on him. 'You touch a white woman and you'll swing for it. You haven't forgotten that, have you?'

Heffner forced a smile. 'Only joking, Mr Ballew, just my little joke.' He studied the man-killer carefully. 'Are you still aiming to follow Newton?'

'I'm still following him, yes.'

'I could ride along with yuh. An extra gun might be useful.'

Ballew shrugged, his face without expression. 'Come along if you want. It's nothing to me, one way or the other.' Which wasn't true. He could put the black man out in front.

'I'll come,' Heffner said. 'I owe him something and I can't wait to get him in my sights.'

5
Sheba's Run

A signboard announced that Raintree had a popula-
tion of 113. The figures were a bit faded so Newt
assumed it might have gone up, or down, since that
count. Despite the name he saw no tree and Main
Street was thick with dust.

The town looked a sleepy place, far from any railroad or telegraph office, and Newt didn't think
Solomon's poster would have arrived before him.

He rode slowly along the street, past stores and
saloons and idlers, wondering if his money would
stretch to a meal for himself as well as Sheba. He
passed a barber's shop and an ironmonger's. Wearing
Lane's old clothes, smelling strongly of sheep, was
anybody likely to offer him a job?

A group of older men sat in cane chairs on the
boardwalk outside the hotel, wetting their moustaches
and talking. They watched him dismount and hitch
Sheba. One of them set down his glass and stepped

down to walk around the mare, studying her with a more than casual air.

He was about fifty, Newt judged, straight-backed with his moustache neatly clipped, ex-military possibly. He wore grey suiting with a string tie and Stetson hat. He examined the mare's teeth and slapped the muscles of her legs.

'A nice piece of horseflesh,' he commented. 'D'you ever race her?'

'No sir.'

'My name's Abbott. I breed horses, and I like the look of this one ... I can offer you, say fifty bucks?'

'Sorry, sir, but Sheba's not for sale.'

'Waal now ...' Abbott looked him over, obviously not impressed; it didn't seem likely he'd offer as much for Newt. 'Seventy?'

Newt shook his head, and repeated, 'She's not for sale.'

'I'd like to see her run against one of mine. There would be prize-money, naturally. And betting.'

'I'm not a betting man,' Newt said.

'Your choice, of course. Tell you what – I'll stake you to supper and a bed, and stabling for your mare. In return, you race her against my choice.'

Abbott paused. 'It's just something to make a bit of excitement. Raintree isn't exactly the hub of the county and sometimes I figure we all need livening up. How about it?'

'I can't think of any reason to refuse such a generous offer.'

A sharp voice cut in. 'What are you thinking of, Dad? Throwing your money away again? Who is this drifter? He smells!'

Newt turned to see a weedy version of Abbott, with a pimply face and a sneer. He was dressed in black shirt, pants and a flat-crowned hat; his riding boots shone and he carried a revolver in a tied-down holster. A would-be gunslinger, Newt thought.

Abbott said, 'Try to behave yourself, Junior. I want you to ride Palooka tomorrow, against this man's grey.'

'Sure, why not?' Junior looked at the Colt .44 stuck in Newt's belt. 'Fancy your chances with a gun, do yuh?'

'I can usually hit what I aim at.'

'Yeah? Waal, if you beat me tomorrow, I'll give yuh the chance to prove it. I don't like being beaten at anything by anybody.'

Abbott said quickly, 'I must apologize for my son, Mr....?'

'I'm mostly called Newt.'

'That's because he's a small frog in a big pond,' Junior said, and laughed.

Abbott and Newt looked at each other. Newt didn't bother to correct the mistake; he'd heard that joke too many times, and it had proved a waste of time trying to tell some people.

'Mr Newt, Junior has been thoroughly spoilt by his mother.'

Abbott pointed along the street. 'Tell the stable-man to take care of your horse and send the bill to me.

I'll have a word with the hotel man while you're doing that.'

'And tomorrow,' Junior jeered, 'I'll show yuh how a real horseman rides to win.' He swaggered off.

Abbott sighed. Newt smiled faintly.

Ballew was not pushing hard. Newton had got clean away this time, but that was how the luck ran. It was his experience that if a quarry wasn't harried, there came a time when a man got careless. That was when Ballew liked to come up behind him.

With Heffner, he'd crossed the river and set off in the direction Newton had taken. Where the mare had scrambled up the bank was clear enough; after that the trail became less clear.

Ballew had not visited this part of the country before. 'D'you know your way around here, Heff?'

'I was this way one time, Mr Ballew. Seem to remember there's a town called Raintree further on, where we can ask.'

'Good enough.'

Ballew didn't want to encourage the black man to take liberties; there was something about him, an air of slyness, that he didn't trust.

Heffner was the sort to brood over some imagined slight and then blow up; likely with the Northern army in the war, he reckoned.

'I want first shot at him,' the black cowboy burst out.

Ballew said lightly, 'Why not?'

It suited him that Heffner took the risk. If he killed Newton, fine – he'd shoot Heffner in the back and return with the stolen horse. He guessed Solomon could be persuaded to pay extra for that.

They rode on in silence, Heffner edging in front. Ballew smiled secretly. He never hurried and he never gave up. He would follow a trail for days, or weeks, or months, wherever it led. An admiring client had once called him 'Mr Relentless'.

He would follow Newton until he caught him up and killed him.

In the morning, Newt made sure that Sheba was well fed and cared for; the brightness of her eyes suggested she was ready to travel. He returned to the hotel and ate a solid breakfast, refusing to worry about weight, but determined he'd have stamina.

He met Abbott and they walked over the course together, as it was being marked out. A range of mountains loomed over the town, sunlight glinting on the peaks, darkness hiding in crevices.

It appeared an impressive barrier to the West, and Newt gestured. 'I suppose there's a way through?'

Abbott said, 'There's no problem if you stick to the through trail, and that's marked. If you try for a short cut, you're likely to find yourself back-tracking. There's ravines and rockfalls aplenty up there.'

Newt nodded and gave his attention to the race-course. It began over a mile outside Raintree, ran the length of Main Street and finished at Dead End Dick's, the last saloon inside the town limits. The track was hard and dusty.

Abbott said, 'I have to tell you that my horse, Palooka, hasn't been beaten, and Junior knows the course. The betting makes him favourite. I've been collecting prize-money and it totals one hundred bucks.'

Newt shrugged. 'Sheba is the fastest horse I've ridden, so you'll get a real race for your money.'

'I hope so. I need to warn you, in case you pull it off, that Junior's a bad loser.'

'Sort of worked that out,' Newt drawled. 'I shan't be holding back on his account. A hundred bucks looks good to me right now.'

Abbott still seemed troubled. 'He's got this idea he's fast with a gun.'

'I don't claim to be fast,' Newt said, 'but I sure am accurate. Fair to warn yuh I've killed a couple of men.'

'Are you accurate enough to wreck his gunhand? His right hand?'

'Always providing he ain't accurate as well as fast – and not many are.'

'It might save his life if he couldn't hold a gun for a while. I'd be grateful – I'll give yuh a new Winchester rifle if you pull it off. I bought it for Junior's birthday but, waal, I figure it's best if he gets over his shooting mania first.'

'I'll do what I can,' Newt said.

A crowd was gathering along Main Street for the big event as Newt brought Sheba from the livery and cantered her down to the starting-point.

Junior was already there, aboard a big stallion that moved restlessly under him, as if eager to get rid of its rider as soon as possible. Newt saw he was wearing his tied-down revolver.

'Are you ready, stranger?' the official starter asked.

'Never mind him,' Junior snapped. 'I'm ready!'

Newt just nodded.

The starter lifted his revolver. 'I'm going to count, "one, two" and on the count of three I'll fire my pistol into the air. That's your signal to go as fast as you can.'

Sheba turned her head to look at the stallion for a moment; she didn't appear impressed and turned back to look straight ahead down the course. Newt felt her muscles tense under his slight weight.

'Hope yuh like swallowing dust,' Junior sneered, gripping his reins tightly. ''Cause you'll be following in my tracks all the way to the finish.'

Newt made no response.

'One, two …' The starter's gun *cracked* and Palooka went forward with a rush. Sheba followed, stretching her legs, neck reaching out; she was on the stallion's heels and pressing hard, her muzzle almost resting on Palooka's rump.

They flashed between wagons filled with cheering spectators, heading for Raintree and the finishing-line. For Newt it was an easy ride and he relaxed in the saddle, just a bit disappointed. Sheba moved like a champion, keeping up easily, yet she made no effort to pass.

Newt kneed her to one side to give her room to pass, but Junior swerved his horse across in front of her, blocking her path.

Newt crouched low, adjusting his neckerchief to keep Palooka's dust from his mouth and nostrils.

The beginning of the town showed and, hoofs pounding, the two horses raced along Main Street.

Whole families lined each side of the street, wildly cheering; there was a blur of excited faces. Those who'd put their money on the stallion were happy and Newt was about ready to forget his dream of easy money.

He urged Sheba forward but still she held back. Then, with the finish in sight, she edged to one side of Palooka and accelerated. The way she went past the stallion was exhilarating; Newt felt a surge of excitement and glimpsed foam coming from Palooka's mouth as Junior slashed him with a quirt.

The burst of speed became a winning run past Dead End Dick's, like an arrow from a bow, that had Junior eating her dust.

Newt didn't need to rein Sheba in; she slowed and turned around and trotted back towards the judge. She'd done this before, he realized. Solomon had trained her to wait till the last minute; that was why she'd been disguised. He must have made a fortune betting on her – and he'd be doubly furious at losing her.

For a moment the crowd was silent, unable to believe Sheba's incredible burst of speed; then they cheered and threw their hats in the air. Newt allowed himself a small smile, suspecting a lot of folk were happy to see Junior beaten.

He dismounted outside the saloon.

The judge was grinning broadly. 'A clear win, sir, and a magnificent finish. It's a pleasure to hand yuh the prize-money. I reckon—'

'I reckon he won't live long enough to spend a cent of it,' Junior said bitterly. 'I warned yuh – you beat me so now you face my gun and I'm the fastest!'

His face was bright crimson but, when Newt ignored him, it turned chalk white. 'You cheated,' he howled. 'You deliberately held back – I reckon you stole that horse!'

Newt looked coldly at him. 'The better horse won – that's all there is to it.'

'Liar! Cheat! Thief!' Junior shook with rage. 'Let's see how good you are with a gun. *Draw!*'

Abbott grabbed his son's arm. 'You damned fool! Even you must know better than to sling lead around where there are valuable animals. You'll wait until Palooka and the grey are taken to the livery.'

Junior turned sullen. 'He cheated, and I'm going to kill him.'

'Perhaps.' Abbott looked despairingly at Newt, who gave a slight nod.

The crowd became silent. The race judge waved people back. 'Give 'em room, folks.'

Men with wives and kids edged away, reluctant to miss the shoot-out, yet eager to watch from a safe distance. A stretch of Main Street was comparatively quiet and deserted when Newt faced Junior.

Dead End Dick had appointed himself referee; a gaunt-faced man wearing clothes that might have been discarded after a trail drive, he said: 'When I drop my hat, gents, go for your guns.'

Junior glared at him, but waited. He had cooled enough to realize that if he took an unfair advantage, public opinion would be against him.

Newt waited, aware of the angle of the sun, now almost overhead. He scuffed his boots in the dust to make sure he had secure footing. His eyes never left Junior's, who stared back with poisonous hatred.

In the silence, a dog howled. No one moved. Newt forced himself to stay relaxed. Junior gave the appearance of posing as a gunfighter, dressed all in black.

Dick held his battered hat high, then dropped it. Junior rushed his draw triggering fast. Newt felt the bullet clip Lane's loose-fitting shirt as it passed.

Newt brought his Colt up, concentrating on his aim; he held his breath and squeezed the trigger.

Junior never got a second chance. Newt's slug smashed into his right hand and the revolver spun from his grasp to fall in the dust.

Junior screamed.

'I'm hurt!' Nearly hysterical, he cried, 'He's ruined my hand!'

Newt stuck his gun back in his belt as Raintree's doctor bustled up. He grabbed Junior's arm to look at broken bones and bleeding flesh, without sympathy.

'You've been asking for it a long time, Junior, so quit bawling like a baby and let me fix that hand for yuh.'

Junior shouted desperately, 'Dad, do something!'

Abbott had as little sympathy as the doctor. 'Get your hand attended to, then we'll talk." He turned away, taking Newt's arm and leading him towards the hotel.

'I'm obliged to yuh,' he murmured. 'Let's hope he's learned his lesson.'

Newt doubted it, but kept his opinion to himself, as he accepted the gift of a new Winchester rifle. He made sure it was unloaded and tried the action, looked down the barrel, noted it took the same ammunition as his Colt.

'Thanks. This is sure some weapon.'

'Will you be staying on?'

'Not for long. When I've got myself some decent clothes, I'll be heading west.'

Newt shook hands with the rancher and stepped along the boardwalk to a store. When he came out he wore a new outfit; his Colt was in a leather holster and a wide-brimmed Stetson was on his head. And there was still money in his pocket for food along the way.

He collected Sheba from the livery. It might have been pleasant to stay in Raintree for a while, but Solomon's poster would catch up eventually – and he didn't doubt that Junior would be more than a little interested.

He rode quietly out of town by a back street, heading for the mountains, as Ballew and Heffner rode in at the other end.

6
Sheba's Leap

Ballew watched the sky, aware of Heffner edging in front of him, as they rode towards Raintree.

The sky had turned a sullen grey that promised a cold autumn; the way Heffner sat a horse told him the black man had not been cavalry. Yet he had the air of a veteran.

'Infantry?' he asked.

Heffner flashed him a smile worthy of a hungry shark, white teeth gleaming against dark skin.

'Sure enough, Mr Ballew, sir ... Northern infantry.' He reached down to bring up a bayonet. 'My favourite for Southern officers. In ... twist ... out. Figured you for a Confederate officer straight off.'

He replaced the bayonet in its scabbard. 'But we ain't at war now, are we?' He laughed.

'No,' Ballew agreed. He could place Heffner now; an ex-slave having a go at his previous owners. 'Just veterans who know better.'

The war was not something he liked to be reminded of. He'd got over it, but his illusions had been shattered in the cruellest way. Of course he'd been young then, but the promised glamour and excitement had turned to barbaric horror as day turned to night.

He still remembered the confusion of smoke, dust and noise; bawled orders and the screams of the wounded lying in their own filth; a narrow creek running red with blood; the carnage.

Cavalry slashing with swords at the necks of men running for their lives; an artillery bombardment that hurled soldiers and horses through the air; the stench of decomposing flesh.

Everywhere savagery, butchery and atrocities; a field hospital filled with the limbless and diseased; a blind boy crying. Villages destroyed, crops burning, troopers with scalps tied to their belts.

He'd seen meat crawling with maggots, the starving gnawing on rats and survivors without hope. And all the time he'd known that, behind the battlefield, profiteers – why did he think of Solomon? – were making money out of short-changing the men fighting for their beliefs.

It would have been much the same for Heffner. Whether you wore the blue or the grey, misery was the same; you ducked and dodged and weaved. You killed. You ran to survive. You learnt that war respected nobody and put yourself first. Emotion dried like spilt blood and you grew a shell, became cold and calculating. If you were an officer you led from the rear because those who didn't survive no longer counted.

Heffner seemed not to have lost his emotional involvement, but Ballew suspected that that attitude had developed before the war. Some negroes had always hated their white owners; the war hadn't changed anything there. He'd need to watch the black man when they finally cornered Newton.

Raintree was smaller than he'd expected and he saw no law-office on Main Street. He passed a blacksmith and livery, a store advertising guns and ammunition, and saloons. He dismounted in front of the hotel and went inside.

'I need a drink,' Heffner said, and headed straight for the bar.

Ballew smiled; another weakness revealed. He walked into the dining-room, chose his seat and sat down. A plump woman appeared with a menu and he said, 'A hot meal, whatever you do best.'

'It's pork chops with mash and thick gravy.'

'Fine.'

From where he sat, back to a wall, he commanded a view of the room; it was big and airy and had been smart at one time; colours had faded over the years and there was a layer of fine dust in places. In one corner an older man talked quietly to a youngster wearing a black shirt and pants, with a bandage around his right hand. The older man appeared calm, the youngster eager to get away.

His food came and Ballew ate slowly and deliberately, his gaze constantly roving the room. Then Heffner came hurrying from the bar, excited.

'Newton was here, racing that mare …'

Ballew noticed that the two men in the corner looked in his direction. He sat quietly, using a toothpick as Heffner went on; 'and he had a shoot-out with some kid.'

The youngster in black stepped across the room. 'You know him?'

Ballew brought the poster from his pocket and unfolded it.

The youngster scanned the picture, mouthing the words 'Wanted … reward.' He exploded, 'I knew it – a killer. Now we can hunt him down and …'

The older man joined them. 'Quiet, Junior. I want to know who these two men are, and why they're here.'

Heffner said, 'That Newton sure enough shot down my boss in cold blood. Never gave him no chance. He's a murderer with a price on his head.'

Junior's father looked at Ballew. 'Is this true?'

Ballew nodded, and asked, 'No lawman here?'

'The sheriff rides this way once in a while. We mostly handle things ourselves.'

Junior said eagerly, 'I'll get Mooney—'

'You won't,' his father said sharply. 'You'll stay out of this.'

'He busted my hand and I want to be there when they nail him.'

'You'll stay out of it,' his father repeated. 'Or I've

finished with yuh. You'll get nothing, understood?'

'Mother won't allow that,' Junior said confidently. He broke away. 'Come on!'

Ballew stood up. 'Who's Mooney?'

'Our local tracker – knows these mountains better than anyone. He'll find him.'

Ballew looked at Abbott, and shrugged. With Heffner, he followed Junior outside.

The news spread quickly; a hunt for a man-killer with a reward at the end of it got the blood flowing. Men on horseback carrying guns milled around in the centre of Main Street.

'Where's Mooney?'

When Mooney arrived, sitting on a mule and chewing tobacco; he appeared to be in no hurry. He had cultivated a fine crop of whiskers.

'First thing, who's paying me for this little jaunt?' he asked.

'Me,' Junior said eagerly. 'I'll pay.'

'Twenty-five bucks.' Mooney waited till he was paid, counted the money, put it in his pocket and buttoned the pocket. Then he looked over the would-be posse.

'You fellers listen good.' He waited until he got silence. 'You keep behind me. I don't want nobody treading on this feller's tracks. When we sight him, you can go ahead – those who are left.'

He spat a stream of tobacco juice as if to comment on the men of Raintree.

'Yippee-i-i, let's get moving.'

Mooney set off, insisting on a steady pace. 'You

won't get far into the mountains if you wear your horse out first.'

Someone said, 'Two to one we don't catch the grey.' Nobody took the bet.

Heffner said, 'Easiest way to bring Newton down is to shoot the horse under him.'

Ballew gave him a mean look. 'You even try that, black boy and I'll drop yuh where you sit. That horse is worth more than Newton. Or you.'

The widow Lane rode into Yuba prepared for trouble. The town had been a cowtown before it grew, and the land was still mostly cow country. And she was responsible for Newt shooting the biggest rancher around. She rode into town with her rifle resting against the saddle horn.

She was glad Johnson was dead, pleased with her hand in it. She'd been attracted to Newt and was glad he'd got away....

Did she really want to go back to sheep-rearing? She had enough money in the bank to start a new flock, but she felt restless.

She rode along Main Street, aware she was being watched, and dismounted outside a small store, with one half given over to woman's clothing. Grace, the storekeeper's wife, who served as the town's dressmaker was her only friend.

'E. J!' Grace's eyes li up as she walked through the doorway.

Grace was an extra large size – the reason she'd

started dressmaking – a jolly woman who liked food, drink and a laugh. She'd had reverses, but nothing seemed to daunt her; her husband ran the store much as she directed.

'I'm sorry about Tom, but rumour says you've got a gunman to kill Johnson. The sheriff's not back yet – you sure ain't aiming to head any popularity stakes. Come on into the back room and tell me about it.'

To a customer she added casually, 'Come back tomorrow. Shop's closed now.'

The woman left hastily, obviously to spread word that the sheepwoman was at Grace's.

'That hat! And those aren't your clothes ...'

As Lane filled her in, Grace busied herself laying the table for a meal.

'You'll stay the night with us,' she said. 'If anyone objects, I'll deal with 'em.'

She closed one hand to make a fist the size of a ham. As she began serving a meat pudding on to three plates, she raised her voice.

'George, food's on the table and we have a visitor.'

Her husband came through from the store, a slight figure with a few wisps of faded hair on his bald head.

'Hello, E. J. Hear you've been stirring trouble again.'

'Not me,' Lane said. 'I just finish it.'

She still found it hard to relax, even among friends. She'd been wound as tight as a spring over Tom's murder. That had been unexpected; threats yes, possibly a beating ... but that Johnson would order his

61

tame gunman to kill had not been anticipated by either of them.

Then had come the shock of the cattle-king's men driving the flock over the cliff edge, and the pain of putting down the survivors. And Newt arriving and killing Johnson. Now …

George said, 'Not every hand is against yuh, E. J. Times are changing and I reckon the days of the big ranches are almost over. The small outfits are switching to fat cattle and homesteaders are putting up wire. Why, we might even get a half-way honest sheriff at the next election.'

He unrolled a poster and laid it on the table.

'Look at this, Grace. It just arrived on the stage.'

Lane caught a glimpse of the picture on the poster; it showed Newt's face and offered a reward.

'See the signature at the bottom,' George said.

Grace's gaze moved down the wording. 'C. Solomon … that crook! Now he's got hold of a railroad!'

Lane felt a twinge of alarm. Grace had told her, more than once, about Caradoc Solomon; he'd been selling claims for homesteads, split into quarter sections. Being crooked, he ran off fake deeds for the same sections and sold those too – with the result that families ended up with nothing for their money. The local law decided that first come, first served.

'Took Solomon's horse, did he? Good for him – I like that.'

Lane was eating without tasting anything, worried.

A two-hundred-dollar reward would attract scum like Heffner. Newt would be hunted mercilessly.

'Anyone robbing Doc can't be all bad,' Grace said, and laughed.

'Serves him right,' George said, nodding.

'It was Newt who shot Johnson,' Lane said.

There was silence. Anyone in Doc Solomon's bad books needed all the help he could get; she forgot about buying sheep. Newt had stood by her and now he needed help. And Heffner had killed Tom. She would stay long enough to outfit herself and buy provisions; then ride to warn him.

As Abbott had said, the trail over the mountains was well marked. Newt allowed Sheba to set her own pace; the ground was rock-hard and mostly uphill. When she paused for a breather, he took in the view.

The air was growing chilly, the sky turning grey. Might even get snow higher up, he thought. He saw rocky crags and peaks everywhere; this was a harsh land with sparse grass and stunted trees. The mountain path just went on and up as far as he could see.

They moved upward again until, reaching a bend with a drop to one side, Newt looked back down the way he'd come. Miles behind he glimpsed, between upthrusting rocks, a bunch of horsemen following.

Someone had organized a posse. He kneed Sheba to encourage her to move along a bit faster.

Although he had a good lead, anyone local would know this trail from experience, and might know short cuts. He kept going, looking behind him from time to time to check the gap between them. The posse was gaining, pushing their mounts.

He wondered what had set them off. Then he caught a glimpse of a black face among his pursuers; Heffner. A reward poster and the black cowboy were a bad combination. Then he recognized Junior, and grimaced. And the one lagging at the rear wearing a derby ... who was he? A bounty hunter?

He tried to figure what was best to do. Even a tracker would have problems on this sort of terrain if he turned aside; but Abbott had warned of dead ends. He might have to backtrack eventually.

He kept climbing, but it was obvious the posse was gaining on him. If he pushed Sheba and she missed her footing he'd be stranded. Reluctantly, he decided to take a side branch and hide, wait them out. It seemed wise to save Sheba's strength.

He waited until he saw a narrow way leading down to disappear around a column of rock. When the posse was out of sight, he turned aside; the surface was bare rock and shouldn't betray him.

It seemed at first that he might be lucky. The way narrowed but showed no sign of petering out. When he heard the clatter of hoofs on rocks, he reined in and waited till the posse passed. Then he went on again.

Around the next bend, Sheba stopped. Before her was a chasm.

There was no way forward; the gap was wide with a

sheer drop for hundreds of feet. Neither horse nor rider would survive that fall – and the far side sloped down towards the brink; its floor appeared cracked and loose.

Abbott was right, he'd have to go back. Then he heard horses and men's voices. One said confidently, 'He turned here. We've got him bottled now – there's no way out.'

Newt turned Sheba to face the posse and unlimbered his new Winchester. As the first rider showed at the bend, he loosed a shot close to his head. The man pulled back in a hurry.

'He's there!'

Another member of the posse poked the barrel of a rifle around the corner and Newt shot it out of his hands. There were sounds of men retreating.

A voice called out, 'Yuh might as well surrender, Newton. We can sit here till yuh starve.'

Newt didn't bother to answer. He had food. It would be thirst that got to him, and Sheba. He went back to look at the chasm. With a run, could she clear it?

It was that or stay trapped and wait for the end. He didn't think Heffner, or Junior, would be inclined to show mercy.

He led the mare forward again, showed her the gap and stroked her head.

'What d'you think, gal? Can you do it?'

The mare was an Indian horse and likely used to mountain trails. She'd shown herself to be sure-footed so far, but the distance was more than Newt fancied. He hesitated, then made up his mind.

He went back as far as he could to get the maximum run, settled himself in the saddle and urged Sheba to speed. The mare never hesitated. She charged headlong for the edge of the drop and stretched her legs.

Newt, clinging to the saddle horn as she soared like a winged Pegasus, caught a glimpse of a long drop and jagged crags waiting for a victim. He felt chilled, and held his breath, praying silently.

The jump seemed endless – as if the gap actually widened – until Sheba's fore hoofs scrabbled at loose chippings on the far side. Newt felt the shock of landing as her impetus carried them forward, sending gravel skittering over the edge.

Her hind hoofs barely touched the surface at the brink as she landed; she struggled for balance, teetering, straining and clawing for a purchase. She almost slipped back.

Newt vaulted from the saddle, grabbed the reins and hauled on them. She recovered her footing and scrambled forward, snorting. Newt started to breathe again.

A howl of rage went up from the far side. Bullets followed Newt as he led Sheba along the track, past an outcrop that sheltered them, and rested a while. There was no hurry. No one was going to attempt to follow them. No one in the posse was feeling that desperate, or lucky.

'That's some horse,' one posseman said admiringly.

'Yep,' added another, 'and the rider ain't exactly the nervous type.'

Ballew glanced at the tracker. 'Is that it? Is there no way around that we can reach him?'

Mooney chewed on a wad of tobacco and shook his head.

'He's got a clear run now. We'd have to turn back and start again.' He considered what he'd said, and added, 'Anyway, I ain't too sure I want to catch up with an *hombre* who'll take that kind of chance. It might not be healthy.'

7
Border Town

'You don't look happy, Doc.'

Solomon said briefly, 'Business worries.' He laid another card and raked in the pool. His mind was not fully on the game.

'He's worried we might take a dollar off him,' one of the players said.

'Some hope!'

The four men were all cardsharps, waiting for the evening session to begin in Damwell's largest saloon. They passed the time practising against each other. Doc was their acknowledged expert and the other three watched eagle-eyed to study how he manipulated the cards.

It was an education to play against this miniature man with snow-white hair, known admiringly by his cronies as the Napoleon of swindlers.

Solomon could cheat with the best of them, but here, he barely kept himself in brandy and cigars.

He'd temporarily promoted one of the railroad men to boss his crew; but where the hell was Ballew?

He'd expected results before now. He wanted to hear that Newton was dead, that his mare was back and ready to race. He'd expected to turn control of the railroad construction team over to the gunfighter. But he'd heard nothing and, stuck here, he was beginning to fret. He'd paid in advance; it ought to have brought results, that was how he looked at it. He needed to get back to the city to do what he did best; charm money out of the get-rich-quick.

He frowned as he won another hand.

If Ballew fell down on the job, he'd have to try something else … and he already had an idea about that.

From the mountain, Newt turned south; it was, he hoped, something his pursuers wouldn't expect. As he drifted along, not hurrying, the air became warmer and the grass greener and he rested Sheba so she could graze.

He slept out at night and followed a river by day until he reached a small town. Swarthy-faced Mexicans clearly outnumbered whites, indicating he was close to the border.

He found a livery and instructed the stable-boy to give Sheba oats in her feed, then entered the first cantina he came to and ordered a meal.

It was chilli-hot and he drank a lot of water with it; afterwards he lingered with a mug of black coffee, wondering what to do. Maybe he should go further

69

south. He'd heard that a lot of wanted men lived south of the border.

He was considering this when the screaming began.

It sounded like a woman, or a child, and had a note of desperation. Newt started to get up, then sat down again, realizing he was in no position to interfere. The screaming finally turned to sobbing and he heard men laugh. He frowned.

Finally he could stand it no longer. He pushed back his chair, went to the door and looked along the dusty street.

A young girl hardly more than a child, clutched at her torn clothing, shrinking back against the wall of a saloon. A half-circle of men pinned her there. She was in tears.

The men were a rough-looking bunch, unshaven and dirty; they laughed as they grabbed at her. Nobody tried to stop them. They appeared to be drunk, and all were white and armed.

Someone shouted, 'Your turn, Al.'

A bearded man lurched towards her, unbuckling his belt. It was too much. Newt moved fast, pushing through the ring of men to use the barrel of his revolver on the drunk's skull. Al collapsed in the dust.

'What d'yuh do that for?' a man asked.

'I don't think the lady appreciated his interest.'

A man with a scar across his face staggered forward, scowling and clawing at his revolver.

'Don't care who yuh are – you can't interfere – this is our town.'

'That's right,' slurred another of the gang. 'Hell, she's only a Mex whore. We were just having a bit of fun, is all.'

Newt stepped in close and jabbed the muzzle of his Colt into a spreading stomach. 'Go someplace else and sleep it off.'

Swaying, swearing, the scarred man reeled away, followed by the others. Newt realized he'd been lucky; if they hadn't been drunk....

He looked around; the girl had gone, so he walked back to the cantina. He was a little surprised; he'd heard that Mexicans were jealous of their women and handy with a knife – yet not one had tried to help the girl.

A bit later he realized the street was deserted; though a few faces peeped from windows in adobe buildings or wooden shacks.

As he stepped inside, the cantina owner said, 'Another coffee, *señor*? No charge to you, but maybe you'd best leave town before the Weedman gets to hear about this.'

'I just got here.'

Newt sipped hot coffee and found himself relaxing. He stared diagonally across the wide street to the only stone building in town, the mission church with its high bell-tower.

For a moment he was reminded of his early life, when he first heard the bells ring and had liked what he heard.

'When do the bells ring?'

The cantina owner sounded sad. 'Never, *señor*. The *Americanos* forbid the ringing of our bells.'

Newt frowned. 'Why?'

A stout Mexican waddled through the doorway, mopping sweat from his face.

'*Señor*, at last comes a man of courage to stand against these *bandidos*. The *alcalde* of San Jacinto welcomes you.'

He brushed back a drooping moustache and attempted a small bow.

'You are staying long, *señor*? Please say you are and I can offer you a job – paid work. Alas, the pay is not high by *Americano* standards but it will be paid. I, Miguel, promise that.'

Newt said, 'I've just been advised to leave town. What sort of job are you offering?'

The mayor looked reproachfully at the owner of the cantina. 'That was not a good idea, José.'

José shrugged, and brought coffee for the mayor. 'I was not thinking, Miguel.'

The mayor sipped the hot coffee with a show of appreciation. 'This gang,' he said. 'These gringos … they are not known by you?'

'I never set eyes on any of them before,' Newt said.

'That is good. They are trouble we do not want. No woman is safe, even in her home. They shoot up buildings, never mind who is on the street. They help themselves to food and drink and anything they fancy in our shops; they pay for nothing, and we are not a rich people.'

'You've got no law in this town?'

Miguel hesitated. 'We had a policeman, a family man ... they nailed him by his hands to the door of the jailhouse. They are terrible men. No one is safe, not even children. I appeal to you, *señor*, as a man of courage....'

Newt smiled faintly.

'You are, perhaps, a man who fights with a gun and is much wanted?'

'You might say so. What's the pay?'

'Ah, *señor*, it is not enough, but you will be paid, say, ten dollars. Of course, there is a bed in the jail – our people will give you a meal, a drink, a little tobacco, *sí*?'

'I don't drink, don't smoke.'

'That is admirable, *señor* and shows great willpower.'

'But my horse needs feeding and stabling.'

'Of course, your horse shall have the best that San Jacinto can provide. A palace! You will accept?'

'Why not?' He'd got to stop running sometime. Newt smiled at the notion; he'd be wearing a law badge if a posse did catch up with him.

José said quietly, 'They are not always drunk, *señor*.'

'I suppose not.'

'And there is the Weedman to consider ...'

Newt looked at Miguel, then back at José. 'What makes this Weedman so special?'

The mayor clapped him on the shoulder. 'Nothing you need fear, my friend. Come, I will show you our fine jailhouse. On the way I will tell you everything you need to know.'

Newt saw José grimace as he moved back behind his counter. He was muttering something under his breath, something that sounded suspiciously like, 'No need to fear the Weedman … no more than the devil himself.'

Ballew was briefly amused. Neither of his companions was in a good mood as they rode west, mile after mile, with no sight of their quarry.

It was beginning to seem that Newton and the mare had vanished from the face of the earth. The prairie remained resolutely empty; the sky was greying over, the air turning chill. Ballew had a premonition it would be a hard winter.

Heffner, slightly ahead as usual, was missing the reward money he believed to be his due. He was feeling cheated and, as a veteran, should have known better. The kid, riding beside him, was another matter.

Junior had obviously been spoilt as a child and hadn't got over it. He still expected everything to be done for him, and must have his own way. He was filled with spite over his damaged hand; each time they halted he practised drawing his revolver and shooting with his left hand.

Ballew encouraged him a little, enough to keep him riding with them. Heffner scowled and swore.

'Why are we dragging this rubbish along? He's useless – can't make a fire, can't cook.'

Ballew drawled, 'Kid's sure keen to be a man-hunter.'

Heffner spat, and turned sullen.

Later on, when Ballew began to veer from the westward trail, Junior asked, 'Why are we going south?'

''Cause it'll be warmer,' Heffner sneered. 'Don't want mama's boy to catch a chill, do we?'

Junior ignored the black man.

'Just a hunch,' Ballew drawled. 'We haven't cut Newton's trail, so I figure he's maybe aiming to cross the border.'

He was guessing, but with the quarry clear away again, it seemed a reasonable guess. He'd lingered to study the mountain chasm when the posse turned back. He reckoned it was a jump that took some nerve, and he would be happier with two men out in front when he finally caught up.

And the mare was a horse in a million. As he rode south he gave some thought to how he might keep the mare for himself – if he could get around Solomon. That wasn't going to be easy.

8
The Weedman

Newt felt a bit strange sitting in his own law-office; it seemed a long way from punching cows. The jailhouse was small, built of adobe and fitted out with a desk, chair and single bed. At the rear was a barred cell that might hold a couple of drunks, three if they were crammed in.

The wooden door still had the holes and brownish stains where the last lawman had been nailed to it. A thought that did nothing for his confidence.

Miguel had given him a metal star in a circle, apparently cut from the lid of a tin can; it had been carefully shaped by a craftsman and a pin soldered to it. Now it was pinned to Newt's flannel shirt.

From being a wanted man, he'd moved to the other side, and wondered how long this could last. Not long, he suspected, if Big Al had his way.

A shriek startled him out of his chair; it was followed by crude laughter. Newt snatched up his Winchester and stepped outside.

Further along the street, a bunch of roughs circled

someone on the ground and were enjoying themselves. The dreadful cry became an agonized moaning as Newt hurried forward.

He came up on them fast, rifle levelled. They had an old Mexican down in the dust and Big Al was grinding a boot-heel into his face. He wore cowboy boots with high heels.

Appalled, Newt triggered to slam a .44 slug into Al's leg, knocking him sideways. Blood spurted from the hole in the Mexican's cheek as Al ended up, cursing, on the ground beside his victim.

Startled, the gang scattered. The one with the scarred face grabbed for his revolver, but changed his mind when Newt swung his rifle to cover him.

'Get out of town and stay out. If I find any one of yuh here again, I'll throw him in jail.'

Scarface laughed. 'You keep wearing that star, feller and I'll use it for target practice!'

Big Al limped to his feet, shouting, 'You, Thorne, help me!'

The scarred man brought Al's horse and helped him into the saddle.

Newt stood over the Mexican protectively as the old man cradled his face in his hands, blood seeping between his fingers. Newt wondered if there was a doctor in San Jacinto.

As the gang turned their mounts to head out, Big Al glared at him.

'Bastard! We'll be back – and the Weedman will have something special for you!'

*

The widow Lane came into Raintree and let her horse drink at the water-trough in Main Street. She kept one ear cocked towards the idlers seated outside the hotel; naturally they'd looked her over as she passed and she'd heard talk of a horse-race with a mare winning. It was a start.

She dismounted and banged the dust from her hat, then led her horse to the livery for a feed and a rub down. She took up her rifle and went to talk to the men outside the hotel. It was as an aid to memory that she casually swung the barrel in their direction.

'Anyone called Newt riding that mare? A real gent would invite me inside to wash the dust from my throat and give me the latest news.'

An elderly man with whiskers stretched himself and drawled, 'My pleasure, ma'am,' and escorted her into the hotel bar.

'What'll it be?'

'A beer will be fine. Better make it a large one. I've been riding all day.'

'Mighty hot,' her escort agreed and spoke to the bartender.

She glanced around. A husband and wife in one corner of the big room attracted her attention; they were arguing, their voices raised.

'It's your fault,' the man insisted. 'You've spoilt him.'

'But you let the man who ruined his hand just ride away!'

'To stop him turning into a gunman. Surely you don't want that?'

'I just want him back!'

'Thanks.' Lane accepted a large glass filled with beer and drank deeply. 'That's better. Now tell me about the mare and her rider.'

The elderly man smirked. 'Don't often get a woman riding into town alone. Reckon you ain't the only one after that reward money.'

'That's possible,' Lane admitted.

'That feller now, sure beat Abbott's Palooka, and Junior got real upset.' Her escort cackled at the memory. 'Newt, that was the name he called himself – got chased by a posse and lost 'em in the mountains. Sure can ride – reckon them two gunnies after him will have their work cut out.'

'One a black man?' Lane took another large swallow of beer. 'Who was the other?'

'Black as coal. The other feller called himself Ballew. Wore a suit and derby – a pro, I'd say. Did you hear that Newt's wanted by the law?'

'Not by the law,' Lane corrected. 'Some railroad crook put up the reward poster.'

''But he'll pay up?'

Lane shrugged. 'From what I've heard of Solomon, I wouldn't bet on it.'

They were joined by the couple who'd been arguing. The man looked to Lane like a successful rancher.

'My name's Abbott, and I've got an interest here.'

Lane gave him an icy stare. 'Cattleman?'

'If it's relevant, no. I run a horse ranch. You say Newt's not wanted by the law?'

She relaxed. 'That's right.'

'He picked on my son,' Abbott's wife burst out.

She had been a beauty in her day, Lane thought, a woman used to getting her own way. Now she was pale with tears dried on her cheeks, and tense. 'He shot Junior in the hand ...'

'Lucky Junior,' Lane said drily. She wasn't really interested.

'And now he's joined those awful men chasing him,' Mrs Abbott wailed.

The horse-rancher looked disgusted. 'He's gone bad. I keep telling yuh – why won't you believe me?'

She tried to beat on his chest with her fists, but he caught her wrists with his hands.

'Stop it! You're making an exhibition of yourself.'

'But I've lost him. My only son, gone ...'

'Your fault. Behave.'

'Where's Newt headed now?' Lane asked.

Abbott shrugged. 'It's assumed he's travelling west, after he cleared the mountain.'

'Maybe.' She hadn't reckoned Newt was slow in the brains department, and he knew he was being hunted.

Lane went to the dining-room and stoked up on beef and potatoes and black coffee. Maybe he didn't know he now had three would-be killers on his heels; she didn't like the way the odds were piling up.

She didn't wait for morning. She collected her horse and left Raintree, following after Newt and the gunmen.

The gang's hideout lay in the hills above San Jacinto, an obscure valley with one entrance that was narrow and easy to guard. Here members of the gang could feel safe enough to make a fire and relax, because any lawman who bothered them wasn't likely to bother them a second time. To provide entertainment, they sometimes allowed a lone man to ride in.

Big Al was cursing as he sucked on a bottle of whiskey, trying to numb the throb in his leg. Even Thorne, with the scarred face, was wary of him in his present mood.

The Weedman sprawled on the ground beside the fire, smoking. Thorne often wondered how he stayed alive. He rarely ate, sipped water from the spring when someone brought him a dishful.

No one could guess how old he was. He resembled a skeleton with skin draped over it, gaunt of face, his ribs showing. His hair had fallen out and the skin around the bones of his fingers was transparent. He'd rather smoke than eat and rarely moved from his usual place.

His final resting place, Thorne reckoned.

He smoked all his waking hours, though it was difficult to tell when he was asleep and mumbling in his dreams, or more or less conscious and living out his visions.

It was because of his visions that the gang bothered with him. His visions were violent; they tormented him so he cried out in horror, shuddering and shaking like a leaf in a gale. It was then they fed him another smoke.

The Weedman's visions were hideous, fascinating and inspiring; they gave the gang ideas beyond the ordinary. Their own notion of violence was straightforward and limited. The Weedman's weren't, so they used his ideas to scare hell out of the people of San Jacinto.

'What d'yuh see, Weedman?' Big Al demanded.

A few of the others gathered round as the Weedman mumbled to himself, his voice barely audible.

'Flames … burning … men with masks … a smell of roasting flesh.'

'Yeah, yeah.' Al was impatient. 'This new lawman – what d'yuh see for him?'

The Weedman went on mumbling, his voice a dreadful whisper, his face like one cast in wax.

'What was that?' Al leaned closer. 'Speak up – louder.'

Thorne felt uncomfortable, and looked at the faces around him, dirty, stubbled, listening as if to a preacher from hell.

No one knew for sure, but it was said he'd been caught by the Apache as a child and lived among them as a slave, that he'd started to use the weed to dull the pain, and now it was a habit.

A habit that could not last much longer – and then what would they do?

Heffner was fed up. Fed up with the long chase after Newton. Fed up with Ballew giving orders.

Above all, fed up with Junior, an arrogant nobody from a wealthy family. He knew that kind well.

He was sick of the whole white race, sick with a hatred that welled up from the past when he'd been a plantation slave. When any delay in obeying an order meant the whipping-post. When he was treated worse than the master's hounds, housed under a leaking roof with only scraps to eat. Kept in poverty, kept uneducated, kept down.

The master race, in their pride, called him inferior, primitive, degenerate. He was tired of being considered an animal and not human by the bigots.

Bitterness became the seed of hate; as he grew up the hatred blossomed into a burning need for revenge. With the war he had the chance to hit back, and he never took a white prisoner.

He smiled at the memory. Now he wanted Newton, who'd cheated him of a well-paid job with Johnson, killing other whites. He wanted to use his bayonet on him. 'In – twist – out'. There was nothing like cold steel to humble an enemy.

He was riding alone, in front, leading the way south, and he twisted in the saddle to look back. Ballew was too dangerous to tackle, much as he'd like to. Junior stuck close to the man-killer, buddying up.

Heffner's lip curled. Junior, yes. Junior would pay for his arrogance.

9
Vision of Doom

'*Señor*,' said the small Mexican boy, '*señor*, there is a *bandido* in the Miramar.'

'That so?' Newt drawled. 'Just the one?'

'*Sí, señor.*'

Newt stood up. The Miramar was the largest saloon in town, and Al's gang had seemed to favour it. Now one of them – why only one? Was it a trap? – had he ignored his order to keep away.

He picked up his Winchester and went to the door of his office and looked out. The Miramar seemed quiet enough, but if he couldn't make his order stick, he might as well take off the badge.

The street was almost deserted as he moved along the boardwalk and the boy, eyes shining in a brown face, tagged behind.

'Is there a back way in?' Newt asked.

'*Sí, señor*, I will show you' The boy confidently led the way down an alley and along a dusty path between

84

empty cans, bottles and boxes. He indicated an open doorway.

'Here, *señor*. Will you kill him?'

'I hope that won't be necessary. I'll just throw him in the jail.'

'Tough *hombre* with a gun,' the boy said.

'So I'm a tougher *hombre*, with two guns.'

Newt stepped through the doorway into a shadowed passage, moving quietly. At the end of the passage he looked into the saloon where Thorne, the one with the scarred face, leaned on the counter, glass in his right hand. His head was turned towards the batwings.

Newt studied him carefully. A holstered revolver hung on his right hip, butt forward, indicating a cross-draw with the left hand. The wooden butt had a well-used appearance.

Newt took in the rest of the saloon in one sweeping glance. Empty, apart from the bartender. The mirror behind the bar had been shot to pieces on previous visits, so there was no reflection.

Newt padded up behind Thorne and slammed down the barrel of his rifle on his left hand. The scarred man dropped his glass and spun about, holding his injured hand. 'You—'

Newt jabbed the muzzle of the Winchester into Thorne's belly, lifted the revolver from the outlaw's holster and shoved it in his belt.

Thorne sucked in air. 'You're being stupid. Big Al will kill yuh slowly for this.'

Newt turned to the bartender. 'Did he pay for his drink?'

The Mexican spread his hands as if the question were ridiculous.

'Turn out your pockets,' Newt ordered and, reluctantly, Thorne obeyed, one-handed. His gun-hand was still painful.

'All of it,' Newt insisted. 'I imagine you've had a few free drinks here before. And you can help pay for a new mirror.'

He waited while Thorne emptied his pockets.

'Right. Now start walking to the jail.'

Thorne didn't like it. He'd been a man others feared; now he had to take orders in front of people he despised. His breath hissed between his teeth, like steam coming from a kettle, but he walked; walked with Newt's Winchester jabbing the small of his back, across the wide dusty street. He was aware of swarthy faces watching him.

Newt said, 'In there,' indicating the cell at the back of his office. After Thorne walked in, he slammed the door and locked it and put the key in his pocket.

Thorne gripped the bars, glaring at him. 'You'll regret this play,' he warned. 'When Big Al hears, he'll be coming fast – and I sure wouldn't like to be in your boots then.'

It was good weed, so why did it depress him? He smoked like an automaton, because he'd always smoked, as far back as he could remember. The weed took away pain and dulled bad memories; it offered comfort.

Sometimes his visions were good, sometimes bad. He could remember when there had been more good ones, positive and cheerful; but now, sadly, they were mostly threatening and gave him the shudders.

He had no wish to hurt anyone. Revenge was only a word and meaningless because he'd been hurt too often and too badly to want that for anyone, even the big man looming over him and demanding a new vision.

The Weedman felt depression as a damp shroud about him, squashing him down into the earth. It felt grey and heavy. But he daren't stop smoking; it was life to him.

Even close to the camp-fire he felt cold. Even as the flames fascinated, darting tongues of orange and yellow and red among the puffs of smoke curling and uncurling like a snake about to strike, he shivered.

The flames dazzled, sunlight off ice. Through transparent wisps of smoke he glimpsed movement. He took a long drag of the weed, deep down into his lungs.

A voice boomed and echoed. 'Tell me your vision – your worst … tell me what I can do to that bastard – tell me….'

It was a voice like a drum, hollow. It penetrated the fog surrounding him, and the more it penetrated, the more vacant became his brain. The voice boomed, each word pounded, the sound overwhelming him.

He lost his train of thought ... he was floating, drifting in a breeze, feet hardly touching the ground. They couldn't reach him now. Perhaps he was a balloon? This was good weed, he thought vaguely, the best and, for a moment, he tasted satisfaction.

Something exploded in his brain and he felt sick with terror. Something was moving, wriggling, out there at the edge of vision. Something sharp was being inserted, twisted. He felt like a block of ice on the surface of the Arctic Ocean, exposed to a lance of sunlight.

A hand was shaking him. His teeth rattled. 'Tell me ... tell me!'

He stared into the fire and saw the savagely cold flames. His tongue came unglued.

'Lurid orange and blood-red streaks and the yellow of vomit, they blossom and dance the death dance, leaping higher. The flames live! Smoke the colour of lead billows rushes wildly like a twister ... see the women and children running, burning, screaming ... guns erupt and people turn to dust ... buildings blacken and collapse. A town is dying ... pillars of dust, dust and doom.'

Another voice sounded. 'That damned lawman – he's got Thorne in jail!'

There was a lot of swearing, heavy breathing, the sound of metal on glass and the gurgle of liquid.

The loud voice came again. 'Why'd he go into town on his own? Let's ride – we'll burn that damned town down around that lawman's ears, and him with it!'

The sounds of violent movement came to him, and the clatter of horses' hoofs and, finally, silence. Silence and loneliness draped a blanket over him as he lay smoking. In the quiet he could relax. This was the best time of all, when he had a weed with no one to bother him.

He could rest and smoke and dream a good vision … and pray for the final peace.

Mr Newton drove his horse and wagon into the yard outside the farmhouse, his heart heavy and his face blank as a stone wall. He'd been into town to sell produce and get things his family needed. It had not been a happy visit and he didn't know how to face them.

He unloaded the wagon without a word, thinking his slow thoughts, unhitched the horse and led him to the stable. Young Russ joined him as he walked towards the house.

'What is it, Father?'

Newton paused. His wife and daughter stood in the open doorway, watching him, and his wife said sharply:

'Cat got your tongue?'

'This,' he said, and put his hand in his pocket to bring out a crumpled sheet of paper and offer it to her.

She smoothed it out to see a picture of her eldest son, and scanned the words.

'I don't believe it,' she said.

Mr Newton sighed and shook his head. 'This is what comes of leaving home. It's in black and white, Mother, the printed word – our Newt shot a man and stole a horse.'

He shook his head again, as if stunned.

Russ grabbed the paper to read for himself. He was taller than Newt, with red hair and a temper.

He snorted disgust. 'It's a lie. Obviously. Newt's been framed. I'll get my horse and gun and go to help him ... see where it says "dead or alive"? And they offer a reward!'

'No, you won't,' Mrs Newton said promptly. 'I'm not losing two sons. You'll stay here and work the farm.'

Russ said, stubbornly, 'I'm going.'

His sister read the poster and frowned. 'What are my friends going to say? You must stay, Russ, and stand up for me. I'll never be able to face them after this.'

Mr Newton still felt troubled, but his mind was now clear.

'I don't like it, but Russ has the right of it. We're a family and stick together. Newt's in some trouble, and Russ has to side him, even if it is hard on the rest of us.'

'Right, Father!' Russ's eyes gleamed. He'd got an old Colt revolver hidden away, and he'd had his own horse since he'd learned to ride.

'I'm away now ... don't worry Mother, I'll look out for Newt, and he'll look out for me!'

10
The Bell-Tower

A guitar played quietly in the back of José's cantina as Newt lingered over his meal of tortilla and goat-meat. Across the street, the bell-tower gleamed white in brilliant sunlight. The bells remained silent.

'Tequila, *señor*?'

'Thanks, but no. Reckon I may need a clear head before long.'

Ever since he'd put Thorne in jail, Newt had expected a visit from Big Al, or the mysterious Weedman.

There was a sudden clatter of galloping hoofs outside, followed by wild yells and gunshots and a scream.

Newt came upright, reaching for his Winchester. He moved to the doorway to see Big Al's gang of outlaws running wild, laughing as they shot out windows and rode up on the plankwalk.

Dogs and chickens scattered as the gang – Newt estimated there were about twenty of them – rampaged the length of the town, shooting at everything that moved. He saw the body of a Mexican face down in the dust.

Newt crouched inside the shadowed doorway, wondering what one man could do. He had his rifle and the Colt, and extra shells, but would anyone in San Jacinto back him up? He needed an advantage.

The guitar had stopped abruptly as José dived flat on the floor behind the counter.

Newt saw a flicker of yellow flame and oily smoke.

'José, they're aiming to burn yuh out!' he yelled.

The Mexican wriggled his way towards the door and peered out anxiously. 'Our lady guard us!' he prayed fervently.

For a moment, smoke eddied and obscured the street and Newt took the chance to dart across, heading for the bell-tower.

One outlaw saw him and charged. Newt heard running hoofs, and dropped on one knee. A chunk of lead whistled past and Newt fired upwards at an angle. The man slid sideways in his saddle and the horse carried him away.

Newt continued his run, reached the tower and pushed open the door; he closed it behind him. When he'd got his breathing under control he went up a wooden ladder to a narrow platform built around the bell. He looked out through a slit of a window.

It was bad down there. Men with flaming torches set wood and shacks alight. As women and children ran from the burning huts, trying to reach the safety of adobe buildings, other outlaws shot them down.

Newt swore, raised his rifle and sighted on a man with a torch; he fired, and the man spun around and sprawled headlong.

A couple of men dismounted and tried to break Thorne out of jail; the key was in Newt's pocket. He fired twice, ensuring that Thorne stayed where he was.

By now, the Mexicans had realized the deadly intent of this latest attack and were beginning to fight back. Desperate men had nothing to lose. The mayor, Miguel, had a shotgun in his hands, while José was urging his fellow townsmen to 'kill the *bandidos*!' The bartender from the Miramar ran out to grab a dead outlaw's revolver.

As Newt reloaded he saw the young girl he'd saved from Big Al dart into the street to snatch up a child crying for its mother. Both were riddled by a barrage of bullets as she tried to reach cover. The child's mother ran screaming at a horseman, hacking at him with a carving knife.

The sweat was like ice on Newt as he lifted his Winchester again. He felt cold, beyond emotion, as he worked the trigger; this gang was no longer human to him, but a pack of mad dogs to be eliminated.

He remembered the words of the widow Lane: 'Remove the king-pin, the rest will collapse....'

Big Al had not yet worked out where the death-dealing shots were coming from. He stared suspiciously at the rooftops as Newt took careful aim and put a slug through his heart.

Still the massacre went on, the gang killing whoever got in their way, Newt shooting outlaws. He saw Miguel reel back as a bullet caught him in the shoulder. There was no mercy as the town burned.

José was hiding behind a water-barrel when one of the gang, his horse shot from under him, staggered on to the boardwalk. José rose up with a machete in his hand and a head rolled.

Smoke drifting across Main Street spoilt Newt's view. Flames crackled and shacks collapsed. He went down the ladder and opened the door to the street, glimpsed one of Al's men with a gun in each hand stalking a wounded Mexican.

Newt whipped up his Colt and fired and the man went down, writhing in the dirt.

Bullets slammed past his head like angry wasps and he dived for cover, triggering fast and reloading. A man doubled over, leaking blood. Another caught a .44 slug in the head. A riderless horse went charging past.

Gradually the noise of battle died as ammunition was used up. The remnant of Al's gang who survived galloped away; Newt didn't think they'd be back.

In the silence, flames roared as wooden huts fell apart; the bereaved began to wail. Suddenly Newt remembered Sheba – in a stable at least partly built of wood. He moved quickly, relieved to find the livery still standing.

The building, close to the end of town, was wreathed with flames creeping closer. The Mexican stable-boy was on his own and obviously scared as some of the horses used their hoofs to batter a way out.

'Let them go,' Newt advised. 'The stable will burn soon, and you can round up the horses later.'

He pulled open the door, keeping well back, as frightened animals bolted. Sheba stood calmly waiting. He saddled her and mounted, tossed the boy a coin.

'If anyone asks, you haven't seen me.'

'*Sí, señor.*' The boy pocketed the coin quickly, as if someone might snatch it from him.

Newt left town quietly. He felt numb and had no wish to face another human being. Anyone following him would, hopefully, assume he was one of the dead; there were enough bodies around. Maybe he could simply disappear.

He headed north into a leaden sky. Presently a wind blew; a wind from the Arctic bringing a threat of snow.

Solomon kept a poker face, even though he was writhing inside and thinking furiously. He took another mouthful of brandy, swallowed, and sucked on a cigar; he could see no way out.

Across the table, in a private room paid for by Doc Solomon, Judge Otis sat smiling.

The judge sipped Solomon's brandy, smoked one

of his cigars and purred with quiet satisfaction. He, too, believed there was no way out.

'A hundred dollars is nothing to a man who owns a railroad. Even if it is the Golden Pacific!' He flicked ash at the floor.

'You're corrupt, Judge.'

'True, Doc. And you're guilty of fraud. You want these investors off your back, don't you? A hundred dollars is chicken-feed – or do you prefer a court action? That could be expensive.'

Solomon fumed inwardly but kept his temper. 'I'm temporarily embarrassed, Judge.'

'Which of us isn't?' Otis had a sympathetic tone of voice. 'At this moment, I have a young woman waiting who is being ridiculously expensive. I need a hundred dollars quickly – you need to stop your investors taking you to court. I'm sure we can deal.'

Solomon said, 'Fifty?'

Otis shook his head sadly. 'So far there are only two investors complaining. Don't wait until there's a crowd. A crowd can so easily turn into a mob, and a mob into a lynching party. I doubt I could hold them back then. And certainly not for a paltry hundred bucks. Now is the time, Doc.'

Reluctantly, Solomon dipped his hand inside his coat and pulled out a sheaf of banknotes. He counted off twenty five-dollar bills and passed them across the table.

'Make sure I'm not bothered again.'

'Of course, Doc,' Otis smiled blandly. 'May I suggest you put on a bit of a show? As if you really mean to

push this railroad clear across the continent. It would
help to convince your investors.'

The judge put away Solomon's money, finished his
brandy and left, closing the door behind him as he
continued to enjoy his cigar.

Solomon poured himself another brandy with a
shaking hand, and cursed the day he'd set eyes on
Newton. It seemed that one thing after another had
gone wrong for him since then. And still there was no
word from Ballew.

He sat hunched over for several minutes, concentrating on his breathing to empty and calm his mind.
Yes, the judge was right; he had to make more effort
to satisfy investors.

Above all, he had to deal with Newton. He would
delay no longer. He'd already decided what action to
take. It would cost money – again! – but once Newton
was dead he felt sure he could buy his way out of
anything.

Ballew reined back his horse and stared into the
distance. Behind them storm clouds built up like a
moving wall of darkness; in front, sunlight shone on a
well-grassed valley. Smoke drifted, obscuring the view.

'Sure enough something burning,' Heffner said.
'Could be a town – reminds me of the war.'

Junior sat quietly in the saddle; he'd learnt that
both his companions were veterans.

Ballew completed his deliberations. 'We'll take a
look,' he said, and urged his horse forward.

Coming down from the hills, it was some time before they reached the ruins of San Jacinto and then Ballew had to agree: it did look like towns they'd burned during the war.

He rode slowly along Main Street, sided by Heffner and Junior. It was a solemn ride, with a bell tolling and the smell of wood-smoke strong in his nostrils. Further on a procession of mourners carried coffins from the stone church to the cemetery.

Junior was amazed; he'd never seen anything like this. Gaps where wooden huts had stood, smoke blackened adobe walls jutting up like stained teeth. Silent Mexicans stared at them as they rode past.

Suddenly, an American voice shouted, 'Hey! Get me outa here, will yuh?'

They were passing the town jail and Ballew slid from the saddle, murmuring, 'A chance to find out what's been going on.'

The door had gone and he walked into the empty law-office to see a man with a scarred face behind the bars of an iron cage. He brought up his revolver and blasted the lock. The door pushed open with some effort.

'Thanks. I'm called Thorne and I thought I was finished – the greasers haven't even given me a drink of water. I just want to get my hands on that lawman, and when I do—'

Ballew interrupted: 'Let's find a cantina. We've been travelling, and you can tell us what's been going on over a meal.'

'I ain't got no money,' Thorne muttered. 'That damned Newt cleaned me out of every last cent.'

'Newt?' Ballew stopped and looked hard at Thorne. 'Now you really interest me – I'll stake yuh to a bottle and a meal.'

They found a cantina that was open for business and ordered, even though the Mexican waiter didn't want to serve the ex-prisoner.

'You had best leave pronto,' he advised, 'before the law arrives.'

Ballew gave him money. 'Is the law still around?'

The waiter shrugged. 'He must be somewhere, even if I haven't seen him since the shooting ended.'

Ballew shifted his chair slightly and eased his revolver in its holster. His gaze moved from the door, to the open window, to the back door.

When their food came, Junior made a face. 'This stuff is smothered in garlic!'

Ballew ignored the side-play, and gave his attention to Thorne. 'Tell me about Newt.'

'That lucky bastard! We ran this town – we helped ourselves to anything we fancied, booze, women, everything – till he interfered. We didn't need money. Then the Mex mayor gave him a tin star and he went stupid. Killed Big Al, and the others ran for it, leaving me in jail. Jeez, if you hadn't turned up, I don't want to think what might have happened. Damned greasers!'

Ballew made a thin smile. Lucky? Stupid? The kid got himself a badge and wiped out this gang; it appeared he was learning fast.

'We're after this Newt,' he said. 'If you want revenge, you can ride along.'

'You bet I will!'

Heffner glowered and mumbled, 'White trash.'

Another body to shield him when they caught up, Ballew thought, and tossed some coins on the table. He left the cantina and walked slowly along the dusty street to where a livery stable had been. A small Mexican boy squatted with his back against an adobe wall, looking downhearted.

'Seen a grey mare?' he asked casually. 'Rider calls himself Newt.'

'No, *señor*.'

Ballew brought a single coin from his pocket and polished it till it shone in the sunlight. He tossed it from hand to hand and the boy's gaze followed it.

Ballew murmured, 'Newt's an old friend of mine.'

'He said not to—'

'He would, wouldn't he,' Ballew agreed. 'I figure he left town, right?'

'*Sí, señor*, going north.' The boy shivered. 'Into the cold.'

Ballew tossed him the coin and returned to the cantina.

'There's no hurry – the mare's had a rest so we won't catch her. Take it easy till morning.'

Thorne hammered the table with his fist.

'And when we catch him, I'll gut-shoot the bastard. I want him to beg me to end his misery. Then I'll walk away and leave him to die – the way he left me in a greaser jail!'

11
Endless Night

If Mack had ever had a first name, he'd forgotten it; and Mack was a shortened form of his family name. It made him difficult for the law to trace.

He was small and skinny and anything crooked appealed to him; his liking for easy money was matched by an aversion to hard work. Or danger.

His favourite trick was waiting in an alley after dark for any drunk to leave a saloon, knock him on the head with his revolver and empty his pockets. Minimum risk, maximum profit.

This new job posed a definite risk, which was why he'd hesitated at first. A grey mare was easy to get and he'd keep whatever money he collected. It was the possibility of murder he was wary of, but somehow he'd been talked into it.

Daylight was fading as he waited behind an outcrop of rock at the bottom of a long and winding canyon. The stage was running late but that was all right; it would be darker, making identification harder.

The mare was skittish and he reckoned to get rid of her quickly after this job. He had his gun out ready, his ears tuned. The driver would be trying to make up time, not watching for a hold-up.

He heard hoofbeats, the groaning of a heavy coach as it rattled over the rough track through the canyon.

He stepped forward from cover to give himself a clear shot as the team showed, tightened his finger on the trigger and the lead horse went down. The other horses stumbled and the coach went over on its side.

The driver tried to jump clear but failed. His head struck a rock. One man crawled from the upset coach, but just sat holding his back, dazed. A woman followed, clutching her purse.

'I'll take that, ma'am,' Mack drawled. 'This is a stick-up.'

'You won't!' she snapped.

Another man scrambled out of the wreckage, gun in hand. 'Leave the lady alone!'

This one, Mack thought, and put a bullet in him. The passenger was knocked backwards, his gun flying out of his hand. He lay still. The woman gave a little scream and held out her purse.

'That's better, lady,' Mack said, snatching it. 'Nobody else need get hurt if you all keep calm and hand over your money. My name's Newton and I've already got a price on my head, so don't tempt me. I've nothing to lose. Now give!'

The other passengers didn't argue, and when Mack rode off into the gloom he was feeling pleased.

He'd collected more than he'd expected and Newton – whoever he was – would get the blame. Maybe he'd do it again. He liked the idea of someone else being held responsible for his crimes. Other hold-up men would be operating too; everyone claiming to be Newton.

The reward on his head would go up each time. Mack laughed; maybe he'd go after this Newton himself and claim the reward!

Newt let Sheba go where she liked. The mare was rested and fed and wanted to run. He just wanted to put San Jacinto behind him; never before had he been involved in violence on such a scale. He'd killed again, and again, and felt sickened. He imagined this was how the war must have been, and just wanted to forget.

He stayed in the saddle from habit as Sheba stretched her legs; his brain seemed to have shut down. The sky darkened and a wind rose. The first flakes of snow drifted down.

At first it hardly registered. He didn't mind; it would cover Sheba's tracks if anyone tried to follow them. Then he realized that night was coming and the temperature had dropped sharply. The wind drove the snow hard against him and the mare veered away to avoid the direct blast.

The cold began to penetrate and his instinct for survival awoke; he stopped briefly to wrap his blanket around him before going on. He no longer had much

idea of where they were or which way they were heading. The sun disappeared and his world became a
curtain of white slapping him in the face; a cold wet
curtain.

Sheba slowed, placing her hoofs carefully. The wind
howled and Newt began to lose the feeling in his
hands and feet. Sharp crystals stung his exposed skin
and he brought his bandanna up over mouth and
nostrils and pulled his hat lower.

When he half-turned to look behind him, Sheba's
prints were filling almost as soon as she made them.

He could see no shelter anywhere. The land was
flat, the short grass covered over; there was no building, no bluff to get behind out of the wind. He saw
only a bleak colourless place that got colder as they
continued.

Newt left it to Sheba; while she moved through the
drifts they might reach somewhere more hospitable.
There was no chance of getting a fire going to warm
them in the open.

The wind raged like an angry thing. The snow came
in great whirling clouds and he froze to the saddle as
Sheba plodded forward. When he looked up, he saw
no stars to steer by.

He began to wonder why he was here at all. Had he,
in another life, really wanted to be a cowboy? He imagined cowhands gathered around a roaring hot stove in
a bunkhouse; but then, who would be looking after
the herd?

Sheba was moving downhill cautiously, feeling her

way through dark gloom and clouds of whirling white flakes. Booming gusts of wind surged, and Newt endured a cold that pierced flesh and chilled bones.

She stopped and he realized she'd reached a creek, frozen over. Laboriously he dismounted, his clothes cracking as he moved, and broke the ice for her. There was running water beneath and she drank her fill. Newt tasted it but it was too cold for him and only made his teeth ache.

He stared at an empty horizonless land blanketed with white and had never felt so isolated. In his imagination, this could only be the end of the world and he the last man alive.

Shivering, he mounted again and they went on. Newt's breath was a cloud of vapour hanging in front of his face. Apart from the moaning of the wind it was a silent world; white flakes landed softly on snow and vanished. Sheba plodded on with her rider clinging to the saddle horn with numb hands.

It seemed an endless night. Newt was frozen and hungry; he couldn't remember feeling so exhausted before, and the empty darkness was scary. He rummaged in his saddle-bag for a strip of dried meat to chew on; it didn't do much for his stomach but kept his jaw from freezing solid.

Sheba moved slower and slower and Newt was barely conscious. He dozed in the saddle, forcing his eyelids to open at intervals, but nothing appeared to have changed. He saw white flakes descending and heard the whine of the wind. Under him, Sheba put one hoof in front of another, stumbling in the drifts.

The white-out frightened him and he clung to the saddle horn as if nothing else existed in this wilderness. He'd never before imagined that anywhere could be so desolate.

Newt drifted in and out of sleep, swaying in the saddle.

A blood-orange sun loomed on the horizon and he shook himself to wakefulness. The blizzard had blown itself out and he stared at a flat white expanse with not another living thing in sight.

Newt felt barely alive; his blood seemed to have stopped circulating and there was no feeling in his legs. He banged gloved hands on his thighs and tried to swing his arms; they felt like lead weights.

He urged Sheba along, no longer aware of much, but he knew that to stop was to die. The glare off the snow was painful, and he was cold and wet; the mare seemed to move ever more slowly.

Newt was almost unconscious when they reached a town. Hands pulled him from the saddle, supporting him, and a voice said, 'Look after his horse.'

Another voice said, 'Better get the doc.'

A third voice came, 'Seems to me I've seen that face – on a Wanted notice!'

Newt was past caring when he was pushed into a cell and on to a bunk. The warmth felt good.

Miguel sat in José's cantina. There was a bottle on the table and each man held a tumbler as they relived the cleansing of their town. A sound of hammering came from outside where a few men, more energetic than most, were putting up a new shack.

Miguel and José sat admiring each other. They were veterans now, survivors, and the mayor kept his wounded shoulder bandaged and his arm in a sling. José touched the machete on the table, wondering how long he could make the rust-brown stain on the blade last if he were careful.

Miguel kept on glancing through the open door, hoping someone would come to praise their fighting abilities.

He saw a lone rider approaching. A white … woman! Astonished, Miguel sat upright. An *Americano* woman? Alone?

He stroked his moustache with his uninjured hand. When she stopped outside and hitched her horse to the post, he got up and waddled to the door.

'*Señora*, I, Miguel, *alcalde* of this town, welcome you to San Jacinto.'

As he bowed, the widow Lane made a small smile. 'I'd like a hot meal and a cool drink. And my horse needs a feed.'

She entered the cantina and sat down as José bustled away to prepare a meal for his unexpected guest.

Miguel called to a small boy, 'See to the *señora*'s horse, pronto.'

Lane poured herself a drink from the bottle the two Mexicans had been sharing, swallowed and sat back.

'Much better!' She gestured to the street. 'Looks like you had yourselves a war!'

'*Sí*, that is so.' Miguel indicated his wounded shoulder. 'I myself led the attack against the outlaws plundering our town.'

José returned with a tray of steaming food, and picked up his machete. 'And I myself removed the head of at least one gringo.'

'Fine,' Lane said. 'I can see you're a couple of macho warriors. Now tell me if you've seen an American on a mare calling himself Newt.'

Both Mexicans stared at her. José said cautiously, 'You are, perhaps, his wife, *señora*?'

'Stop putting ideas in my head. He was here then?'

'*Sí*,' Miguel said. 'I made him an important man by giving him the star – a badge of the law, you understand?'

Lane nodded. 'I get it. He broke up this gang for yuh. So where is he now?'

José looked sheepish. 'Riding north, *señora*, into the storm. Not wise.'

'On the other hand,' Miguel said, 'he might avoid those following him.'

'Like a black man, and a kid with a bandaged hand?'

'*Sí*, you know them. And the man in the derby …' The mayor crossed himself. 'Very bad man, I think, such cold eyes. There is no soul there.'

They all had another drink, and Lane ate her meal.

Miguel said, 'And there is also Thorne, remember?'

He turned to Lane. 'Your Newt put one of the gang in jail. The men following him freed this Thorne, and he rides with them.'

'Four to one now,' she murmured. 'The odds are building up. He's sure going to need help when they do catch up.'

José murmured. 'That won't be soon. The snow will hide his trail.'

'You could be right.' Lane went to the door to study the sky. In the north, heavy grey clouds were beginning to clear – and she really must rest her horse.

The morning would be soon enough. She'd follow Ballew, and he would lead her to Newt.

12
Jailbreak

'A waste of good food,' the deputy said, putting down a tray in Newt's cell. 'Pity you didn't die in the storm and save the town money.'

'I'm grateful,' Newt said politely. 'It is good food. Compliment your wife for me, please.'

He was feeling better, well enough to worry about Sheba. 'My horse. I hope she's being looked after.'

'Naturally. An animal like that is too good for the likes of you.' The deputy was young, starting a beer belly and seemed in awe of the sheriff, expected from the county town any day. He continued to grumble.

'The doctor says you'll live, but I say, why bother? A waste of time, effort and money. Soon as the judge gets here, you'll be tried and hanged. But I'll stick to the rules.'

'I'm grateful,' Newt repeated.

'If you hadn't killed that passenger on the stage you might have got off, but not now.' The deputy shook his head.

'What passenger?' Newt demanded. 'What stage?'

'You ain't trying to deny it? Not after you boasted who you were, and what you've done. Hell, you'll hang for sure.'

'It wasn't me,' Newt said.

The deputy snorted disbelief. 'I found this when I searched yuh.' He held out a star in a circle, cut from tin plate. 'You didn't kill a lawman either?'

Newt almost smiled. 'No, I was appointed lawman in San Jacinto.'

'You going to try that one on the judge?'

The deputy went out, slamming and locking the door after him, and Newt settled to tackle beef and hash browns. Being in jail sure beat freezing in a blizzard, but he was beginning to wonder how he was going to save his ...

'... neck,' Thorne said viciously. The scar on his face was livid. 'This I want to see – that bastard at the end of rope with his legs kicking air. It'll have been worth the ride just to see that.'

Heffner showed his teeth. 'Yep sure enough, that'll be a purty sight.'

They sat around a table in one of the town's dining-rooms, stoking up after an unpleasant ride through snow-covered country. It was only Ballew's insistence that had kept them moving along.

Now, because he'd followed the same small creek Newt had followed, they'd reached the same small town – to learn their quarry was in jail and waiting for the circuit judge to bring him to trial.

Junior was happy too, but had another problem. 'I wish I could figure a way to get my hands on the mare.'

Ballew decided to encourage him. 'If you can, she's yours, kid,' he said, and smiled. If Junior got his hands on the mare, he'd soon take her for himself.

It was the deputy he concentrated his thoughts on; that oaf was claiming the reward the stage company had put up. Ballew guessed someone else had been smart enough to lay the blame on Newton, and scowled.

He'd been chasing Newton ever since Solomon had paid him – so why should some beer-swilling deputy get anything?

Russ's horse was reluctant to go much further. He had to admit he'd pushed the animal too hard early on, in an excess of enthusiasm. He'd been disappointed not to join Newt quickly, but it seemed his brother kept on the move.

He worried, too, about reports of hold-ups and murders by 'Newton'. He couldn't believe his brother was involved, and the way the amount of reward money kept going up was alarming.

He was fed up and, following a winding track between timber, wondering where he could rest and feed his horse, when a rider appeared in front of him; a slight man on a grey horse pointing a gun at him.

'Just throw your purse on the ground and you can ride on your way.'

Red-headed Russ glowered. He could feel his temper coming to the boil. He was annoyed with himself because he should have been more alert.

'And suppose I don't?

'Waal, I guess I'll have to put a slug in yuh and help myself. You've maybe heard of me, name of Newton? I'm a desperate man with a price on ...'

Russ felt a surge of blinding rage. This was the murderer putting the blame on his brother, someone he could take out his frustration on.

He kicked his horse into a sudden motion and charged full tilt at the hold-up man. His mount's shoulder slammed into the would-be robber, taking him by surprise. The revolver fired into the air and the slight man hit the ground, the gun flying from his hand.

Russ leapt from his horse and landed heavily on top of him, knocking the air from his lungs. His hands went around the robber's throat and tightened their grip as if they had a will of their own. The man under him struggled wildly but couldn't break the stranglehold.

Russ, furious, bawled, 'Blame my brother, will yuh? You murdering, lying, thieving rat!' He shook the limp body as if it were a child's doll.

He got no answer and realized he would himself end up a murderer if he didn't allow this crook to draw breath. He forced himself to relax his grip.

'What's your name?' he demanded furiously. 'Why are you putting the blame on Newt?'

The man lay there, weakened, gasping like a fish hooked out of water. 'Mack ... not my idea ...'

'What d'yuh mean, not your idea?'

'He put me up to it – "call yourself Newton", he said.'

Russ felt a red haze coming over him; his fingers tightened automatically. 'Who said? Tell me who said that, you lying dog!'

Then he had to relax his stranglehold again, so the man under him could get enough air into his lungs to answer.

'Jeez, man, you've got a grip like a vice. Take it easy so I can talk. If I name him, will you let me go?'

'Why should I? You're a—'

'He's got it in for your brother. Killing me won't change that.'

Russ began to see that Newt's best chance lay in getting at whoever had hired this crook.

'All right. Tell me the name and you can ride – but I'll be reporting this to the law as soon as I hit town.'

'Yeah, waal, this ain't my usual game ... guess I'll travel some.'

Russ brought up his old Colt and placed the muzzle between Mack's eyes. 'The name, damn you.'

'Doc Solomon! It was Doc who put me up to it.'

Russ let him get up. Mack went to pick up his gun but Russ said, 'Leave that. Just ride.'

Mack hoisted himself in the saddle and used his spurs.

Russ Newton picked up Mack's revolver and sat on

115

a tree stump, breathing hard. He forced himself to relax. He was still shaking. He'd lost his temper before, on more than one occasion, but never before had he come close to killing anyone. It was a hard lesson and he'd badly scared himself.

Newt finished his evening meal and sat on the edge of his bunk. Pacing up and down only used up energy without achieving any useful purpose. It appeared there was nothing for him to do but wait for his trial.

He hoped he'd be allowed to speak in his own defence. The deputy, at least, seemed an honest man, even if he wouldn't listen.

Evening clouds gathered beyond the tiny barred window, bringing shadows to his cell. The deputy was still in his office because Newt could hear small movements. He thought about Sheba, concerned that she might not be getting the attention she deserved.

He was starting to feel fit again, but needed exercise – if he ever got the chance. His ears pricked as he heard another voice from the office, the squeal of a shifting chair and a heavy thud.

A bunch of keys came between the bars and clanked as they landed on the stone floor. A dim figure moved back.

'Who's there?' he called.

No one answered and Newt remained still, waiting, listening intently. What was going on? He called again, 'Is anyone there?'

Again he received no answer. What had happened

to the deputy? Who had given him the keys, and why?

He felt suspicious, but decided to take a chance. He picked up the keys and tried them one by one till he unlocked the cell door; he eased it open quietly and stepped into the office.

The deputy lay on the floor, unmoving. Newt knelt and felt for a pulse. Only knocked out, which was a relief. He could do without being blamed for the murder of a deputy sheriff on top of everything else.

He wondered who his rescuer was, but not for long. He saw his gunbelt hanging from a wall-peg and strapped it on, picked up his Winchester and Stetson. A desk drawer provided two boxes of ammunition. He moved to the doorway and peered out.

Main Street was quiet as dusk gathered, almost empty. Yellow light shone from a saloon further along; a big store was shutting its doors. Darkness was closing in, doorways gloomy with shadow.

He waited, forcing himself to be patient, watching the street, trying to make up his mind. He decided to find Sheba and moved on to the boardwalk.

He glimpsed a painted sign: LIVERY STABLES, and headed towards it. To reach the stables he had to cross a patch of oil-light shining from a window.

As soon as he was in full lamplight, a cold voice spoke from deep shadow.

'Stop right there, Newton! Drop the rifle and raise both arms and surrender to me!'

13
Surprise Meeting

After the snow stopped, Lane easily tracked Ballew and the others on Newt's trail. But the snow was deep and the going slow; when she reached the small town the sun was sinking and she felt cold right through.

She hitched her horse, walked into the hotel dining-room and ordered hot food. The few men gossiping over coffee around the fireplace had the look of travelling salesmen, and she listened to their small talk as she ate.

'Hear they got that stick-up artist in jail.'

'Yep, a bad one that – appears he shot a lawman.'

'Waal, unless the judge arrives soon, I'm going to miss the hanging.'

'Not much doubt there. Calls himself Newton, and boasts about what he's done.'

Lane's lips curled. Not very likely, she thought. Why did some men have to believe every rumour that came their way? She reflected, not for the first time, that it wasn't women who were the gossips.

She knew she was prejudiced, but so few men seemed worth anything. Tom had been one. Newt another. Tom was dead, and that part of her life behind her. She had a debt to pay, and Newt was worth saving. She struggled with a new feeling; it was more than a debt now.

Life had to go on, and Tom had never been the jealous kind; he wouldn't want her to shut herself away like a nun. Yes, she intended to save Newt from Ballew and his crew, but she still felt young and the juices flowed. Though he didn't know it yet, she was going to save him for herself.

She finished her meal and paid, and led her horse to the livery to feed and bed him. She picked up her rifle and walked along Main Street towards the jailhouse.

A young man passed her, moving in the opposite direction, and she paused; his face reminded her of someone. She looked back; young, dressed in black, his right hand bandaged. It had to be Junior, she thought, and watched him enter the stable.

The others must be here somewhere, she realized, and walked on, alert.

It wasn't long before she spotted the black cowboy of Johnson's, and was tempted. She hadn't forgotten who shot her husband but this was a strange town and, apparently, the law held Newt in jail. She could wait.

Heffner was with a roughneck with a scar running down one side of his face: Thorne. Together they pushed through batwings into a saloon.

So where was Ballew? She had no doubt he was the king-pin.

She continued slowly along the plankwalk towards the law-office and jail, watching both sides of the road. Close by, a man in a suit and derby loitered in shadow. Ballew. What was he waiting for?

Lane turned aside, casually, to look into a store window, watching his reflection. In the twilight, shops were closing and workers heading for a diner or saloon.

Ballew waited till there was nobody looking his way, then walked through the open door of the law-office. What was he doing? Lane waited, tense. He was inside only a few minutes, when he came out he moved into a dark alley.

Seconds passed. Ballew made no move and Lane waited. Then Newt looked out warily from the door-way. Finally he stepped outside and walked towards the stable.

As he entered a patch of yellow lamplight she saw him clearly and heard a voice ring out: 'Stop right there, Newton!'

The widow Lane raised her rifle to cover the dark-ness where Ballew hid.

'... and surrender to me!'

A bullet winged past Newt and knocked the derby hat off the head of a man in deep shadow. Ballew turned to face whoever had fired – and, unexpectedly, Newt stepped in close and hit him with the barrel of his Winchester. Ballew sagged, and Newt hit him again.

As Ballew staggered and fell, a horseman came riding along the street. Light flared when saloon doors opened and men looked out to see who was shooting whom.

Newt recognized Sheba. He put his fingers in his mouth and gave a long shrill whistle.

The mare's ears went up and she came straight to him at a gallop, bucking her rider loose. Junior hit the dusty road on his injured hand and howled in pain.

Newt grabbed the saddle horn and swung himself up, snatched the reins and turned Sheba around. Men poured into the street, yelling and firing off revolvers, and he urged Sheba to speed and headed out of town.

Lane waited as men darted about firing guns and running in circles. Newt swept away up Main Street and vanished into the gathering darkness.

Someone grumbled, 'That's Newton getting away,' but nobody felt a need to give chase in the dark.

An old-timer muttered, 'He's heading into the desert, so why bother?' The crowd drifted back to continue their drinking.

Lane crossed to the law-office and stepped inside. The figure on the floor groaned as she lit an oil-lamp.

'Let me see,' she said brusquely, and moved the lamp closer. The deputy pulled himself upright and slumped into a chair.

'Yep, a nasty gash, but nothing a doctor can't fix, leaving yuh with only a headache.'

She felt relief; a dead lawman would have been

another complication. Obviously, Ballew hadn't wanted to rouse the town till he got Newt outside.

'Hit me with a revolver,' the deputy mumbled. 'Feller wearing a derby.'

'His name's Ballew – and you're lucky. I put a bullet through his hat, so I reckon he's gone by now.'

She crossed to the door and looked out. The crowd was dispersing and she saw no sign of either Ballew or Junior.

She bawled, 'Bring a doctor here, somebody!'

When she turned back, the deputy was staring at an empty cell.

'Goddamn it, with the judge arriving any time, and maybe the sheriff too … my head hurts like hell … that Ballew used my own keys to set him free.'

'Not to help Newton,' she said grimly. 'I reckon he was set to gun him down till I took a hand.'

'Pity yuh …'

A figure walked through the doorway and, for a moment, she imagined Newt had returned. But this one was taller and had red hair.

Lane stared. 'Thought I was seeing things. You must be Newt's … brother?'

The youngster nodded. 'My name's Russ, and I'm looking to help him.'

'Me, too. Lane.'

Russ said, 'I heard about the stage. Feller called Mack did that shooting, and put the blame on Newt by using his name.' He tapped his second revolver. 'He won't be doing that again.'

122

The deputy held his head in his hands. 'I don't care. Just go away.'

Lane and Russ were leaving when a doctor bustled in with his black leather bag.

'Right, who's shot?'

The widow Lane touched Russ's arm and jerked her head. 'Come on. Ride or eat first?'

'My horse needs a break.'

Together they walked to the nearest dining-room and Russ ordered steak and potatoes. Lane took a coffee to keep him company.

'Newt saved me when a bigheaded rancher tried to run me off my land,' she said, 'so I owe him one. That's where the black, Heffner, comes from. He's just gone on Newt's trail.'

Russ nodded, eating hungrily.

'It seems that after that, Newt saved a whole bunch of people in a Mex town by getting rid of a gang of outlaws. Thorne – the one with a scarred face – was with 'em, and he's another after your brother.'

Russ ordered a double helping of pie.

'Junior, a spoilt brat, got hurt when he picked on Newt. He's just a vicious kid, but still dangerous. Then there's Ballew – a pro. I figure he was following Newt before he got to me.'

Russ cleared his mouth. 'It was Doc Solomon who got Mack to pretend to be my brother.'

'Solomon again,' Lane said. 'That one's got the nerve of a brass monkey. You finished?'

Russ grinned. 'Except for a bucket of coffee!'

Men came clumping into the diner, calling for the special. They sat at a nearby table, talking excitedly.

'Newton didn't get clear away – there's fellers chasing him. Four strangers, bounty hunters likely.'

'So?' The one with an off-white moustache removed a wad of tobacco from his mouth, wrapped it carefully in an oilskin, and put it in his pocket. 'He won't get far that way. Just desert, and beyond that, a ghost town called Goldwater. A hideout for outlaws who shoot first and don't ask questions afterwards. No posse with any sense is going to follow him far.'

Lane shifted her chair to face the expert. 'Surely there's a way around this desert?'

'Sure is, ma'am. Just takes longer is all. And then what? Still no place to get het up over.'

Lane and Russ left.

'In the morning,' she said. 'When your horse is fresh, we'll take the long way round.'

He nodded.

The railroad depot at Hide City was no longer busy since the cattle towns had moved further west. But the sheds were still useful; the main line passed through and Doc Solomon's spur line started there. The local newspaper was promoting the idea of changing the name to Hide Junction.

Young Charlie thought Golden Pacific a joke, but kept that to himself. He'd learnt locomotive driving from old Vic, who'd been a top railroad man before drink ruined him. Now Vic was Solomon's chief engineer.

Charlie watched, trying not to be critical, as an ancient locomotive clanked slowly, reluctantly, to a halt and Vic climbed down from the cab.

'Brakes still ain't working right,' Charlie remarked.

Vic ignored the comment till he'd taken a swig and passed the bottle. The young engineer was clean shaven and wore a smartly pressed overall.

Charlie wiped the neck of the bottle and drank; he'd take a drink when he wasn't working.

Vic said 'Just old, that's all. The brakes'll hold.'

Old like you, Charlie thought sadly, past it. Vic's overall was stained with his breakfast as well as oil and dirt.

He knew the brakes wouldn't do; knew that a chief engineer of a real railroad would condemn this old workhorse.

'Old is too kind, Vic. Doc bought that engine at scrap price.'

'It still runs. That's all Doc needs. He likes to say, "faster, faster". Plenty of room to stop anyway.'

'Maybe.' Charlie grimaced at an unpleasant memory. 'Maybe, Vic. But not always, not in an emergency.'

14

Prosecution Witness

As soon as he reached the edge of town, Newt turned off the main track. Shadows closed around him and he reined Sheba back; the one thing he couldn't afford was to have the mare put a foot in a hole. He didn't know where he was, and night was coming.

He reached a clump of trees beside a tiny creek and stopped to fill his canteen with fresh water. The air was still warm and he let Sheba move on. The land was empty as far as he could see, the grass dying, and he heard no sound of pursuit.

Who had helped him? When the voice challenged him he recognized a derby hat, so that one was still on his trail, it seemed. Was he a bounty hunter? But someone had shot at him. Who? His escape from jail appeared a mystery, but he was happy to be free again.

When the moon rose he saw he had started to cross a desert towards, on the distant horizon, a range of

126

low hills. He allowed Sheba to decide their pace. The hours passed and the air grew chill. He rested the mare for ten minutes and went on again, alternately riding and walking beside her.

With sunrise, the air warmed quickly and, before long, the heat became almost too much, and Sheba slowed to a walk.

The landscape was mostly a sandy flat, with scattered rocks and cacti. By midday the build-up of heat set the air shimmering.

Sometimes the hills appeared near, then far away. He saw a stretch of water, smooth as a mirror, that unaccountably vanished as he stared at it.

He wiped sweat away and tipped his hat lower to shield his eyes from the glare. This was the nearest he'd been to being baked in an oven.

Further on he came across hoofprints in the sand and set Sheba to follow them, hoping this other rider knew where he was going. The intense heat increased and he wet Sheba's lips with water from his canteen.

She moved slowly but she kept moving because there was no shade anywhere. The sky made a clear blue bowl and there was only the burning sun and silence.

Presently he saw a dark form stretched out on the sand; as he rode closer, buzzards rose and circled above him. Their meal was the body of a horse, and Newt paused briefly, reading sign.

The horse had been shot, and footprints led away across the dust. He assumed the horse had gone lame and the rider had had no choice. He wondered how long ago this had happened.

As he went on, the buzzards settled again; soon the bones would be picked clean.

The heat scorched and Newt had to use all his willpower to resist emptying his canteen in one gulp. The valley floor was cracked where clay showed through, and there were patches of salt.

The man on foot ahead of him made a set of wavering prints where he struggled to remain upright; then came long slurred furrows of sand where he'd fallen and crawled. But he hadn't given up.

Presently Newt saw a body ahead of him, collapsed on the ground; there were buzzards overhead, so he wasn't dead yet.

He pushed Sheba a little and slid from the saddle. The man was face down, so Newt turned him over and moistened his lips with a little water.

The man stirred and opened his eyes and Newt adjusted his hat to cover his face; he still clutched a rifle.

'Horse lamed,' he muttered, as if someone might blame him.

Newt nodded, and gave him a little more water; it seemed to revive him. 'Think you can stand?'

This brought a faint smile and an effort to rise. Newt helped him, and he unfolded a lanky body and clutched Sheba's saddle. 'One, two …' Newt hoisted him up.

He was, Newt realized, an older man, his face lined

and the colour of walnut; there was a revolver strapped to his waist.

Newt sent Sheba forward and walked beside her. The hills didn't seem quite so far away, or was that another mirage? He plodded on, the sun beating down, fighting his need to drink. Sheba came first, or not one of them would survive.

Dust shifted over the dry and wrinkled land. He stumbled on volcanic debris, a prickly cactus stung him. It was like walking through a nightmare until the stranger croaked: 'Pump up in hills … Goldwater.'

Newt roused himself, realized that the desert was really ending and there was hope. A track, with a few weeds, led upwards.

The one good thing about the situation, Ballew thought, was that with the deputy out of action, no unofficial posse was likely to pursue a wanted man into the desert; and that gave him a free hand.

His fancied superiority had taken a double blow; someone had put a bullet through his derby, and Newton had surprised him by using his rifle as a club. He still felt tender.

By the time he'd recovered, Newton had gone. His first action had been to tongue-lash Junior to quieten his noise, and then get him off the street by sending him to fetch Heffner and Thorne.

Whoever had shot at him was no longer around, so Ballew faded into the night.

Heffner and Thorne, when they left the saloon, were not happy; Newton had got away, and the mare was headed into the desert. Ballew made them wait for moonrise to have enough light to follow Newton's tracks in the sand.

Junior started in complaining again. 'That's the second time he's busted my hand, and it still hurts. What I'm going to do to him when I ...'

His voice carried a frightening viciousness, but that didn't stop Heffner from jeering.

'Why don't yuh shut your jaw, baby? Your whining sure enough gets on my nerves.'

The black man was disgusted at the escape; he was thinking Ballew wasn't so great after all. Maybe he and white trash could split the reward between them. Junior was a nothing and easily disposed of.

They took it easy to save their horses, threading a way between dunes.

Thorne squinted at the horizon, and said, 'When we get to the other side, there's a hill track going up to an old mining town, empty now. He won't get much help there. If anyone's home, it'll likely be friends of mine.'

'Anyone I know?' Ballew asked.

'One in particular,' Thorne said. 'Calls himself Cleaver.'

'I've heard of him,' Ballew admitted. 'Never met him.'

Thorne smiled wolfishly.

After sunrise came the heat; blistering heat that had the horses panting.

130

Junior found the sweat evaporated from his skin as soon as it formed. He felt all the moisture was being drained from his body. He complained.

'Jeez, I need a drink bad. I've never known heat like this.'

'Drink all you want,' Ballew warned, 'but when it's gone, you won't share any of ours.'

The land was parched and cracked and the glare came off salt-pans with dazzling brilliance. Further on, buzzards feasted on the remains of a horse; they passed at a discreet distance to avoid the smell.

Ballew paused to study the tracks again. 'Looks like Newton picked up a survivor. Two men on a horse, so we needn't hurry.'

'Guess he won't survive for long,' Heffner said. 'Best if we kill both of them.'

Thorne smiled at Junior. 'There's a pump in the old town at the top. Guess you can use it first if you want.'

Heffner laughed as they rode on towards the hills.

At the end of the track, where the ground levelled out after the climb, Newt saw a collection of half-ruined buildings scattered like discarded toys. Dust piled up against any wall still standing; the only sound he heard was the wind whistling through gaping doors and windows. It was difficult to imagine Goldwater had been a busy mining town only a few years before.

'The pump,' the lanky man gasped, pointing.

It was a straight up-and-down iron handle but, to

Newt's surprise it had been oiled not long ago. Even outlaws needed water.

Newt set to pumping. At first nothing happened then a rust-coloured flow started, and then ... like magic, crystal-pure water.

He filled his hat to let Sheba drink, then he filled his canteen and passed it to the man he'd brought out of the desert. Finally, Newt stuck his head under the pump and took a long swallow.

Vegetation was sparse and Sheba drifted away, looking for grazing. Newt sought the shade and sprawled out. The lanky man sat with his back to a wall, rolled a cigarette and lit it. He inhaled deeply, his eyes glinting with new energy.

'Feel a lot better. I'm obliged to yuh.'

He sat quietly, smoking, studying the layout of the town, the way the wind shifted the dust, the lack of footprints. Finally he looked across the desert and laughed.

'All that way for nothing,' he said ruefully. 'Lost my horse, and could have lost my life if you hadn't happened along.'

He fashioned another cigarette and lit up, then gave his attention to Newt.

'My name's Fisher and I'm a federal marshal. I had a tip the man I'm after might be hiding out here. It's well known as an outlaws' nest. Cleaver is his name on my warrant and he's a killer.'

Newt tried to keep his face blank as he stared at a lined face the colour of leather. He had no doubt this marshal was both tough and experienced; he'd saved the life of a lawman. In other circumstances he might have laughed.

'Newton,' he said reluctantly.

Fisher regarded Newt with interest, squinting through smoke. 'I've heard the name. I have to say you don't look the part.'

'I get blamed for what I haven't done.'

Fisher nodded. 'You're not the first. I ain't got your name on a warrant, so I don't feel obliged to do anything.'

Newt felt relief; he could never have gone up against a United States Marshal. As sunset brought evening shadows and a cooling breeze, he began to talk. 'It started with Solomon …'

'Solomon I know of by reputation,' the marshal said. 'A slick operator we'd love to get a handle on. He's ruined good people and caused a lot of grief.'

When Newt recounted what he'd overheard, Fisher asked: 'Are you prepared to go into court and repeat this under oath?'

Newt nodded. Maybe with this officer he had a chance to clear his name.

'Then I found this man in a derby on my trail.'

'Ballew.' Fisher shook his head. 'He's not just a bounty hunter, he's a killer for hire. You've got serious trouble if he's after yuh.

'Junior … yeah, waal, I've seen so many of these kids. They push their luck till someone finishes them. Meantime, they can be a nuisance. Heffner sounds more serious, one of those blacks with a white chip on his shoulder. Thorne I've heard of... Used to run with Cleaver at one time. You've sure been collecting some bad arses as you go along, Newton.'

Before the light failed, Fisher scanned the desert with some care.

'Figure we can sleep tonight, but we'll spell each other. Our visitors may be early tomorrow, so we'll need to be up before dawn. I'll take first spell.'

Newt got his head down.

15

Gunfight at Goldwater

Sheba pushed at Newt with her muzzle as first light stained the horizon.

'That's a bright horse you've got there,' Fisher drawled. 'Take a look across the desert.'

Newt rose quickly. Riders. One, two, three, four, he counted.

Fisher put out his cigarette, buried it in dust and smoothed it over. 'Not a posse is my guess. Reckon your hunters have caught up. Waal, you're a witness for the prosecution and under my protection – and under my orders.'

His gaze roved over derelict buildings.

'No sense in offering ourselves as targets. Likely we'll see only three of them. Ballew's too cagey to show himself till he moves in for the kill, so let's get under cover.'

A breeze was already shifting the dust and starting to hide signs of their camp.

'Choose a house where you can climb up inside and see the pump,' the marshal said. 'That's our ace – they've crossed a desert and will need water. Keep in mind I'm afoot and need a horse.'

He disappeared through the sagging door of a half-demolished building.

Newt slapped Sheba on the rump and murmured, 'Go feed somewhere out of the way, there's nothing for yuh here.'

As the mare moved away to forage, Newt picked a building across the road from Fisher, so the water-pump lay between them. He climbed what remained of a ladder to the top of an adobe wall and lay flat, cradling his rifle. The building had once had a second storey but now it was open to the sky.

It felt good not to be running any more; even better to have someone on his side at last.

He waited patiently, gaze fixed on the point where the trail came over the crest of the hill. Sheba was out of sight and wind-blown dust had covered their tracks. With full light, the day's heat began to soar.

Newt lay still as a lizard, sighting his Winchester, checking his Colt and ammunition. His water-canteen was within easy reach. He tipped his Stetson forward to shade his eyes, and waited.

Minutes passed. Junior was the first to show, on foot and leading his horse; he gripped a revolver in his left hand. Heffner and Thorne were a little way behind and still in the saddle. He saw no sign of Ballew.

The black cowboy motioned Junior forward. His

words carried clearly. 'There's the pump. See it? I told yuh you could use it first. Go on, help yourself.'

Junior stumbled forward, trampling weeds. His flat black hat was covered with dust. He was reaching for the pump handle when Fisher called, 'Throw down your gun, kid!'

Junior ignored the warning and whirled about, firing with his left hand in the direction the voice came from. His horse bolted. Behind him, Heffner and Thorne dismounted hastily, the black man drawing fast and triggering.

Junior collapsed, shot in the back. Newt, watching Heffner's face, saw a gloating expression and knew the bullet had not been accidental.

Thorne shouted, 'Is that you, Cleaver?'

Fisher called again: 'You are firing on a federal marshal. Throw down your weapons.'

Heffner and Thorne used their horses as shields as they withdrew to cover, loosing off shots at random. One slug whined past Newt's head.

Fisher was right, he realized; the water-pump was the key. The gang needed water and he and the marshal controlled access to it.

Junior stopped his noisy writhing and lay motionless. So young a life wasted, Newt thought and decided that, sometime, he would return to Raintree to tell Abbott how his son had died.

He still saw no sign of Ballew, and that worried him. A silence stretched. There was no movement.

Newt rested quietly, noting the layout of the small

town. He could see most of it from his vantage-point because of collapsed walls; there were discarded tools, rusting iron sheets, boards across the opening of a shaft, part of a big wheel.

A hat appeared around a corner of one of the few buildings that still had a name posted: ASSAY OFFICE. A target to tempt him to reveal his position. He smiled and refused the bait.

He took a small sip of water from his canteen as the heat of day built up, and wiped the sweat from his forehead as he kept his rifle trained on the pump in the centre of the empty street.

The widow Lane took the lead without making it too obvious. She liked Russ but he was still green; she was older and had more experience. The path that wound around the desert was easy enough to follow though it covered many extra miles.

He talked easily about his parents and sister and their farm, but it was obvious it was Newt he admired.

'He's still safe, you reckon?' he asked.

'I reckon. Newt's a survivor if I ever saw one. He'll still be around when we catch up and, when we do, you leave Heffner for me.'

He glanced at her. 'Guess you don't like cowboys.'

'True, but Heff is an especially bad one. A back-shooter.'

She was impressed by the red-head. He'd dropped everything to come to help his brother out of a tight spot. Some families she'd known wouldn't have lifted a finger. And they were farmers. She thought she wouldn't mind joining the Newtons.

There was grazing and water along the way and she kept their pace easy. During the worst of the heat she rested their animals in the shade of some trees, listening for sounds of battle. She rode on when moonlight showed and, by dawn, the hills were close.

Russ heard it first. 'Gunfire!' he shouted, and didn't wait. He pushed his horse to a gallop and she followed.

At the top of the hill they came on the deserted mining town by the back door, Russ in the lead. The main street was thick in dust and weeds grew where the wooden sidewalks had rotted and splintered. For the moment, the shooting had stopped and it was eerily quiet.

Russ saw the man in the derby gliding silently from one bit of cover to the next, intent only on stalking his prey. He slid from the saddle, drawing his revolver.

Young and impetuous, he moved into the open and shouted, 'Drop it – you're covered!'

Ballew whirled, spraying lead, and Russ stepped backwards hurriedly, tripped and fell. He sprawled on the ground, exposed and helpless.

Newt stared in dismay when he saw his young brother step into the open to challenge Ballew. He groaned, 'No!' and dropped his rifle. He leapt from the wall, landing off-balance, and grabbed for his revolver.

Ballew swung around, eyes cold as marbles, and

Newt guessed he wasn't in the same class as the professional. Desperate, he tried a trick, shouting, 'You're not good enough. I've got yuh!'

Ballew hesitated fractionally between the two brothers, then winged a snapshot.

Newt felt the lead tear at flesh as he centred the Colt .44 he had won from Solomon and squeezed the trigger.

Ballew never got a second shot. His expression changed to incredulity as a bullet smashed into his chest. Newt had taken the time to aim and he was dead accurate.

He sank on to one knee, still covering Ballew, and toppled over.

Lane had sworn as young Russ rushed into action. She followed as close as she could, swinging from the saddle to take cover behind some rusting ironwork.

She saw Russ trip, and Newt leap to the ground to face Ballew, and fall. Wounded only, she prayed.

Heffner crept stealthily forward. He had a bayonet in his hand and obviously thought he had two easy victims to finish off. Two whites.

The black cowboy hadn't seen her and she had a clear view of his broad back.

She remembered him shooting her husband from behind without warning, and raised her rifle. She took careful aim and fired twice.

Both slugs struck Heffner in the centre of his back and flung him forward to land face down in the dirt. He tried to crawl away but managed only a few yards before the strength left him and he collapsed.

Fisher was puzzled by the intervention. One of the newcomers appeared to be a woman, but any help was welcome. He tried to see where Thorne was hiding, worried for his witness.

Then he saw the gunman. He was obviously intending to get away, making a grab for the mare to escape on. The mare resisted and Thorne snarled, his scarred face ugly with frustration. He brought up his revolver and aimed at her.

Fisher lifted his rifle and fired once and Thorne went down. It was over.

Fisher stepped outside, holding up his badge of office. To avoid any misunderstanding, he called out, 'Federal law!'

The woman and the red-haired youth were converging on Newton where he lay on the ground. He joined them.

Newt tried a weak smile. 'Russ ... just a scratch.'

Then he passed out.

16
Solomon's Insurance

Although Newt's wound was not serious, Lane insisted on boiling water to clean and dress it, and he found that even a flesh wound could be painful.

'Stop whinging,' she snapped. 'You told me it's only a scratch.'

The marshal took command. 'Round up the horses, will yuh, Russ? Water them one at a time.'

'Are you arresting Newt?' his brother demanded fiercely.

Fisher smiled and shook his head. 'Reckon he's more sinned against than sinning. He's going to be my star witness to put Solomon away.'

Lane looked up. 'I know people who will cheer on that day.'

Fisher cooked a meal and Lane insisted on resting a full day. No one objected.

Newt relaxed easily among friends. He found his

body reluctant to bend, and wasn't sorry to be ordered to rest while the others took it in turns to attend to the chores. For the moment he felt handicapped.

After their meal they drank coffee and Fisher rolled a smoke and lit up. There was some casual talk, and then Russ turned to the marshal.

'It was Solomon who put Mack up to impersonating my brother.'

Fisher nodded. 'It figures. My guess is he's the one who hired Ballew, to shut the mouth of a witness.'

Newt dozed on and off. It felt good not to have to remain alert all the time. Words passed over his head as he drowzed.

Doc Solomon, he thought, if it hadn't been for him … maybe he should go back and see him face to …

Fisher was speaking. 'I want to put Newt in protective custody until Solomon is brought to trial.'

'Or you could leave him with me,' Lane suggested.

Russ added, 'I'll take him home.'

Newt felt irritated. How was it everyone else knew what was best or him? He knew he'd grown up after his recent experiences, knew he owed Doc Solomon something….

As he dropped into a deeper sleep, a resolve was slowly hardening; he must go back alone and face down the railroad promoter. This thing between them would never be settled until he'd done that.

The man who sometimes called himself Cleaver sat quietly and alone in the biggest saloon in Hide City.

He sat at a corner table with a small beer and a pack of cards, playing patience. A rifle was propped against the wall close to hand, and those who knew his trade left him to himself.

The Last Longhorn had few customers early in the evening until a bunch of young cowhands arrived. They lined up at the counter and demanded whiskey. After a few rounds they began to look around for a way to liven things up. They saw Cleaver.

Perhaps they didn't realize his size as he sat quietly laying one card on top of another as if an earthquake wouldn't disturb him. His coat glittered where gold thread ran through it, his white shirt had frills and he wore jewellery. His hair was a silky blond and tightly curled.

One of the cowhands approached, sniffing. 'Is that scent? Perfume?'

Cleaver ignored him, laying his cards down carefully, one after another.

Another cowhand swaggered up. 'Jeez, he smells like a whore!'

Cleaver looked at him. 'Some of my best friends are whores,' he said, and rose in one smooth movement; big-boned and broad-shouldered with an ugly face and full red lips.

He picked up the nearest cowhand and tossed him at the other one. Both hit the floor.

Regulars scattered and the barman ducked through a curtain into a back room. The rest of the cowhands decided here was their night's fun and rushed him.

Cleaver got his back to a wall and picked them up one at a time as they reached him. He used the first one as a club to hit the next. A few heads cracked and blood ran freely.

The cowboys staggered to their feet. They'd had a drink and were slow to learn. As they came back for more, Cleaver grabbed a chair and swung it. The first chair disintegrated and he caught up another.

By the time the barman returned with the sheriff and a couple of deputies, the cowhands were bruised and bleeding and reeling among overturned tables, ruined chairs and broken glasses. One, sitting in a pool of whiskey, looked as if he needed the attention of a doctor.

The sheriff was fat, his deputies young; all three levelled shotguns.

'First man to draw a gun is the first to join the other failures on Boot Hill,' the sheriff said.

They stared at him. 'Only a bit of fun,' one muttered.

'You've had your fun. Now start walking.' The sheriff paused and looked at Cleaver. 'Sorry you were disturbed, Mr Cleaver.'

Cleaver nodded slightly and took up his rifle. 'Boys will be boys, Sheriff,' he said, and walked outside.

He moved casually along the boardwalk and entered the hotel as Doc Solomon was coming out. He tipped his hat.

' 'Evening, Doc.'

' 'Evening, Mr Cleaver.'

He ordered a hot bath and laid out a change of clothing on his bed, wondering at the need some men felt for physical violence.

Moonlight was bright when Newt opened his eyes, wondering what had woken him. He recognized his surroundings, and the ghost-town seemed quiet enough. Even the wind had dropped.

Not far away, the marshal and Russ lay asleep in their blankets. The widow Lane was a bit further off, and snoring.

He heard a small sound and a shadow loomed. A wet muzzle touched him.

'Sheba – good girl.'

He struggled to his feet and stroked her. Fisher opened one eye. 'Trouble?'

'No trouble,' Newt assured him. 'Just Sheba come looking for me.'

The marshal turned over and was instantly asleep. Newt remembered his decision to seek out Solomon and finish it.

He moved Sheba away from the sleepers, quietly saddled her and walked her for a while before mounting. The mare went like the wind and Newt sat easy, enjoying the ride.

He rode through the night, once passing a herd of steers. A solitary cowboy rode around them, singing a lullaby, and Newt smiled; had he really imagined that was the life for him?

With dawn, he reached the town of Eden and

stopped at a livery to buy the mare a feed of oats; and, as he dismounted, felt suddenly weak. He realized his wound was leaking blood.

The stableman gave him searching look. 'Got yourself shot?' He jerked a thumb. 'Our doc's at the third door along – likely still at breakfast.'

Newt steadied himself; he moved carefully along the boardwalk, and knocked. The door was yanked open by a young man.

'Yes? Can I help?'

Newt guessed he was new by his eagerness.

'Come into the surgery.' It was a bare room, with a table and one chair. 'Sit there while I get hot water.'

The young doctor returned promptly with a steaming kettle as Newt removed his shirt.

'A gunshot wound. I'm supposed to report this to the town marshal but that can wait.'

The doctor cleaned and dressed his wound. 'You need to rest twenty-four hours. I suggest a room at the hotel and sleep. That'll be one dollar.'

Newt smiled and said, 'Thanks.' He paid, returned to the livery and resaddled Sheba.

'D'yuh know where I might find Doc Solomon?'

The stableman shrugged. 'Know he's got an office near the depot at Hide City. Can't guarantee he's there now, but maybe. Doc's something of a travelling man.'

Newt climbed into the saddle. 'Which way?'

The stableman pointed and watched till mare and rider were out of sight. Then he crossed to the marshal's office.

147

'I figure that was Newton just left town. Sure looks like his poster. Asking for Solomon.'

The marshal stood up. 'So long as he's left. I don't reckon to tangle with a gunfighter of his reputation. I'll send a telegram to the sheriff at Hide City.'

Doc Solomon was not pleased. He sat in his office at the railroad depot after the sheriff left, a scowl on his face. He took a long breath, wondering if the fates were conspiring against him.

The sheriff had shown him the telegraph form from Eden. Newton was on his way, looking for him. He cursed Ballew. So much for gunfighters; all talk and no action. And, obviously, the marshal at Eden had declined to act.

From disappointment, his mood turned to fury. How could an innocent like Newton, straight from the farm, get away from Ballew? It was hardly possible. Somehow he had to trap this idiot who seemed possessed of the devil's luck.

He needed bait for a trap. Nobody could resist an offer of easy money; call it compensation. He poured a brandy while he gave serious thought to how he'd offer the bait, lifted the glass to his lips … and paused. He needed a clear head; but he needed a drink even more. He sipped slowly.

All he had to do was lure Newton close enough. He pulled out his hidden derringer, checked the load, checked the action. No problem.

Then he remembered Cleaver was in town. Cleaver

was a killer for hire and surely it wouldn't hurt to take out a little insurance?

He lit a cigar as he considered how best to deploy the man-killer.

The widow Lane kept her lips tight-pressed as she rode, with Russ and Fisher, after Newt. She had the feeling that, if she opened her mouth she would say something she would regret later. It seemed incredible Newt could have saddled and ridden away without one of them hearing something.

They rode fast and together until they arrived at Eden, and stopped at the livery; the mare had been noticed and had gone on.

Lane swore when she learnt from the doctor that Newt's wound had re-opened and he'd been told to rest.

Russ made a beeline for the nearest dining-room and ordered meals for three, while Fisher visited the town marshal.

He returned, bleak of face, with a copy of the message sent to the sheriff at Hide City.

Only Russ seemed happy. 'Don't you see? It's a challenge he couldn't resist. Of course he's going after the man who framed him!'

Lane snorted. 'How like a man – the usual macho nonsense. So he walks into a trap, weak from his wound and slowed down … a trap set by a tricky cheating bastard like Solomon. He needs his head reamed out and a brain inserted!'

Fisher looked thoughtful. 'On the other hand, with his usual luck, he may just save the county the cost of a trial.'

The evening in Hide City had not yet swung into its nightly action with drinking and gaming. The horizon still held a red glow in the west.

At the end of Main, where the railroad depot lay silent in shadow, an oil-lamp gleamed in the office of Golden Pacific.

Doc Solomon and Cleaver came out and walked quietly to a shed where the continental rail switched to a spur line. The big door lay half open and an iron monster loomed inside.

Doc laid a proprietary hand on it. 'This is the one, Mr Cleaver. It'll have steam up and the engineer will be ready to drive it as soon as he sees me come out of the office.' He spoke confidently. 'You'll be up in the cab with Vic.'

Cleaver's nose wrinkled. 'It's filthy.'

'I'll get Vic to clean it.'

'Is he reliable?'

'Reliable as a driver, yes. Vic's an old souse and I own him. He won't bother yuh any. You'll be moving slowly, hidden by the iron side of the cab. Likely no one will even see where the shot comes from. I'll be out in the open, close to the rails when I meet Newton. All it takes is one shot.'

'Two,' Cleaver said. 'Two to make sure.'

'His eyes will be on me,' Solomon said. 'A cinch.

150

Nobody expects a gun aboard a locomotive. A complete surprise.'

'Till something goes wrong,' Cleaver said.

'Nothing will.'

Cleaver held out a manicured hand, rings sparkling. 'You pay me now, Doc.'

Solomon put his hand in his pocket and brought out a well-stuffed wallet and counted off notes.

Cleaver thrust them into his own pocket and walked away, disappearing into deep shadow.

Doc Solomon smiled. This time, he thought grimly, not even the devil's luck could save Newton. He had no chance at all. The trap was set, waiting for the mouse to walk in.

17
End of the Line

Vic was in a bad mood, already at the bottle and swearing under his breath, when Cleaver walked into the shed carrying a rifle. Vic was furious that he'd been told to clean the locomotive's cab.

He sniffed loudly as the gunman climbed up into the cab. 'Jeez, d'yuh bathe in that stink?'

Cleaver regarded him with an amused expression. 'At least I bathe, old man. I suppose it would be a waste of time if I suggested you wear a clean overall?'

Vic glared, trembling. An engineer was like the captain of a ship; his word was law. He deserved respect.

'Is this old clunker ready to travel?'

'I've got steam up. We're ready to roll when I see Doc give the signal.'

Vic didn't want to be in the cab with this one. He climbed down and carefully poured sand on the rails in front of the driving wheels.

Cleaver nodded approval. 'You just do what Doc wants and ignore me.'

'Coward,' Vic muttered. 'Hiding behind an iron shield. Shooting from cover.'

'Be careful, old man. This is what your boss wants. It's what he's paying me for.' Cleaver rested his rifle on the iron frame of the cabin and sighted along the rail track. 'You drive, that's all. When I've shot twice, increase speed and take me to the end of the track. I've a horse waiting.'

Vic's lips curled. Best to ignore him. He climbed back into the cab and looked out.

It seemed ages before he saw Solomon waddle from his office. 'Now!' He released the brakes and opened the throttle; the wheels turned and the locomotive began to roll forward, slowly gathering momentum.

Newt rode into Hide City and headed towards the railroad depot at the end of Main. He had mixed feelings; glad it would soon be over, apprehensive that Solomon was too crafty for him to beat.

Shops and stores were open and the plankwalks were busy; but the town was no longer important the way it had been. He saw boarded-over windows and doors, and heard a distant locomotive letting off steam.

He passed a newspaper-office and the hotel, where idlers looked at him with more than casual interest. He didn't stop at the livery. First things first; if he gave Solomon time to get organized, he might meet any number of unpleasant surprises.

He came to iron rails that reminded him of the end-of-line camp where he'd met Cassidy, and saw a signboard: GOLDEN PACIFIC. He dismounted, armed and ready for a showdown.

Sheba waited patiently beside the track.

A railroad man studied him, then hurried into the office. A few minutes later Doc Solomon stepped outside.

He was alone and looked no different from Newt's first meeting with him; short and overweight with a mop of silver-white hair and a ruddy complexion. He could have passed for an elderly cherub. He wore a smile as if it were his badge of office and held out his arms in greeting. In his left hand, prominently displayed, was a sheaf of banknotes.

'Compensation, Newton, a little compensation for all your trouble.'

Newt remained wary, hand on the butt of his Colt .44. He glanced quickly around. A crowd was forming, but well back.

'My dear boy,' Doc said, beaming. 'I'm so glad you've come to sort out our little misunderstanding. It was my fault. I admit it.' He might have been greeting the prodigal son, newly returned. 'I was afraid you might hold something against me!'

He chuckled, moving closer, banknotes extended.

In the background somewhere a locomotive's whistle sounded, and Newt was conscious that they were both near the track.

Doc seemed genial and without any obvious

154

weapon. 'All is forgiven, my boy,' he boomed. 'Faults on both sides, no doubt, and here is a little …'

His voice died away as his gaze took in Newt's horse – a grey mare without markings – and he belatedly recognized the mare.

His jovial expression vanished and his face turned white and then red. His voice became a screech. 'That's my horse – *mine*!'

He lurched forward to snatch at the reins; his other hand pulled out a hidden derringer. Banknotes spilled from his hand and a breeze scattered them.

Newt read triumph in his eyes; the trap had sprung and Solomon was so close he couldn't miss.

He heard a heavy locomotive rattle over joints in the track, sounding like a death knell.

But as Solomon reached for Sheba, she reared up in resentment and lashed out with her forehoofs. The derringer was knocked skyward and Solomon stumbled backwards. The crowd surged forward to scramble for the money he'd dropped.

Fisher, closely followed by Russ and Lane, cantered down Hide City's main street. Men were hurrying towards the railroad depot, including the sheriff and two deputies.

'Something's started!'

A locomotive's whistle wailed, and the lanky marshal spurred his horse forward, forcing a path through the crowd. He saw Solomon stumble backwards as Sheba reared up.

Newt stood alone, exposed, as twenty tons of iron

steamed along the track.

Sunlight glinted on the barrel of a rifle in the engine's cab, a rifle aimed at him. Fisher recognized the face over the rifle: Cleaver.

He brought up his gun and fired a snapshot ...

Newt reached up to grab Sheba's reins to haul her back as the locomotive ground inexorably nearer. He heard a bullet buzz past like a hornet and turned to see Fisher, gun in hand.

He turned again as Solomon tripped on the near rail and fell across the track directly in front of the locomotive. A warning shout went up from someone in the crowd. Doc Solomon tried to rise, and fell back. The massive wheels kept turning, slowly, relentlessly....

Vic never heard the sound of a gunshot above the noise of the engine. He saw Solomon sprawl across the tracks, try to get up, and fall back. He made a grab for the brake as Cleaver fell against him, the rifle dropping to the floor.

'Get away, you idiot!' he snapped, then saw that the back of Cleaver's head was missing. He felt suddenly sick and sobered fast. He grabbed the emergency brake too late.

He knew Charlie had been correct; the brakes wouldn't hold. The engine slowed but didn't stop.

He heard Solomon scream once as he was dragged under the cow-catcher; the scream chopped off abruptly as a driving wheel hit him and kept going.

Newt stood frozen as the scream ended. He felt ill

and turned away, still holding Sheba's reins. He thought, numbly, must get her to the livery.

He saw Russ and the widow Lane forcing their way through the crowd still picking up money. Fisher was showing his badge to the sheriff.

Lane watched Newt carefully. 'You look like yuh need a drink.'

'I don't—'

'Right now, that's what you need,' she said firmly. 'Russ, see to the mare.'

'Sure thing.' For some reason, his brother was grinning broadly. 'And then I'm going to get something to eat.'

'My friends call me E. J.,' Lane told Newt as she led him into the nearest saloon, 'but you call me Eliza-Jane. Your running stops here. I've got the land and we'll build a ranch together. That's what you set out to do, isn't it?'

'You mean, marriage?'

'Of course I mean marriage. What kind of woman d'yuh think I am?' She addressed the barman. 'You got anything like champagne?'

'Like,' he admitted, and poured two glasses of something fizzy from a bottle.

She handed Newt a glass. 'Let's drink a toast.'

'I thought you were against cowboys,' Newt said.

'Still am,' she said cheerfully. 'A toast to our sheep ranch!'

157